Long ago, Lindh lost his wife to a fellow Guardian. Taking vengeance into his own hands, he was betrayed by his Guardian brothers. He left, taking his twin children to live on the surface world.

Trillian, a grandson of Neptune, has received permission to stay on land for one year to learn the skills he always dreamed of as an artist.

Neither man expected to find each other.

Neither expected to find love — life's greatest masterpiece.

Life's Greatest Masterpiece
Copyright © 2023 Deja Black
ISBN: 978-1-4874-3835-7
Cover art by Angela Waters

Published by eXtasy Books Inc.

Look for us online at:
www.eXtasybooks.com

LIFE'S GREATEST MASTERPIECE
MEN OF NEPTUNE 3

BY

DEJA BLACK

DEDICATION

To my editor, my greatest champion.
Thank you, Debbie.
You give me hope.

To parents taking care of families, working, and writing.
You're my freaking heroes.
Every one of you.

CHAPTER ONE

For Lindh Hali, being a chef rather than a Guardian of Neptune had its advantages. No one knew he was a merman besides his children and loyal soldiers. Well, except for Batair, his close friend, confidant, and brother of the sea who first knew him as Lanh Seamus. Lindh had used that name when he moved to the surface to escape detection by any trouble that might have followed him.

It had been years, and the only battle he faced now was in the kitchen of Iliona's Sea Haven—his restaurant, the namesake of his lost love—or with his twins Coralia and Adamaris. Well, sometimes, the occasional human who'd had too much to drink. And the only commands he gave to his faithful Guardian soldiers Dorian, Azizi, and Edra were for meals to be prepared and delivered to the tables. It was a life he loved.

Did he miss life beneath the surface? If he was honest with himself, sometimes. But along with missing that life was grieving the mate violently taken from him years ago. He would not return there, even if Neptune ordered him home.

Lindh walked into his restaurant, pulling a fresh hand towel through his fingers with thoughts of tonight's menu on his mind. He loved this place and had worked hard to ensure people had a place to feel at home, relax, and spend a little time with friends and family. Customers were seated at the carved wooden bar beneath the stained-glass chandeliers, each displaying a creature from his beloved ocean. Spinning sharks hunted a school of fish on one while a purple octopus slid its long tentacles over and under the golden lights of another. Each round table boasted a group of people savoring meals he'd designed himself, the seafood fresh and delicious. The laughter he heard while people talked and ate, telling stories and meeting new friends, filled his heart.

Lindh had a new idea to work on for his menu. He craved new flavors, sometimes savory with sweet, other times tangy and rich. A barrel of fresh apples waited to be peeled and cut for a grilled fish taco bowl with green apples and guacamole. His daughter Coralia was partial to green apples, so Lindh had to admit to being biased when deciding what he would serve as this week's special. He made his guacamole from scratch, everything fresh and ripe.

"It's a packed house, Tetra Lindh," Dorian said, his voice like sanded oak. He was big, not as broad or tall as Lindh. Still, Dorian was a presence here that none could ignore. He'd accepted his place at Iliona's Sea Haven rather than the battlefield.

They all had. Lindh was blessed to have people as loyal as his soldiers to share this life. He had a family, one he'd brought with him and those who would never leave him behind. Dorian, Edra, and Azizi had dropped everything, leaving their people to follow Lindh and his children. Times had been hard at first, but they had each other and endured. He would forever be grateful to them.

"How many times have I asked you to leave that title behind?" Lindh growled.

"Too many to count, but you'll always be the head of our Guardian troop to us. You'll always have our respect as our leader, no matter where we travel," Dorian responded.

Lindh sighed. Arguing about it was futile, he knew. It had been years since he felt like a Guardian and even longer since he felt like Tetra Lindh. Here, his life was about family and his people, not being the arm of Neptune and the protector of all the god viewed as worthy. So rather than rehash the argument, Lindh focused on the people filling his place.

"Yes, it's packed, but then it always is." Lindh peered outside to the line beyond the entrance.

"A blessing, that." Dorian smiled warmly.

Dorian's statement couldn't be more true. No matter how tired Lindh was or how much his feet ached before he went to sleep, the restaurant allowed him to live well. His children, now adults and studying in college, wanted for nothing. They often spent their evenings at the restaurant helping, sometimes encouraging him to take a night off, which was rare. He enjoyed his life, his work, and the people who came to his restaurant. Another diner was simply an addition to his personal coral garden.

"I'd best find my way back to the kitchen to deal with these apples you've left us." Dorian laughed as he headed for the kitchen.

"I was going to do that." Lindh had figured he'd be the one peeling all those apples.

"You could, but who would check the tables and do the visiting you're known for as the host? None of us want that job. So that leaves you, Tetra." Dorian slapped his back companionably and walked through the double doors to the kitchen.

Lindh laughed, the sound rumbling through the room. He'd gotten better at modulating his tone over the years — less creature and more human — though he sometimes slipped up. A few heads popped up, looking for the source of the sound because his voice carried, no matter how much he adjusted it. When they saw it was him, some gazes lingered with interest, and others renewed their conversation punctuated with bites of their meals. Lindh nodded to those who continued to stare, smiling kindly at the blushes that appeared.

Lindh turned away, unprepared for the golden man standing before him. His eyes, an unnatural green, were wide and almond-shaped, and white-blonde hair fell from his crown and flowed over his shoulders. He was slim with a toned body Lindh surprisingly wanted to touch. He caught himself before doing just that but stepped closer to breathe him in.

The man stood furtively between Coralia and Adamaris, looking like a young sea creature who wanted to escape the determined clutches of his two children. How they'd captured the wayward urchin, he had no idea. He could explain to the unfortunate man that avoiding his dynamic duo was hopeless. They had their prey right where they wanted him . . . standing before their father. His twins often tried to play matchmakers for him.

Coralia dragged the man near, and Lindh almost thanked her out loud.

"Look, Dad! We found him at the market. His name is Trillian. Isn't he lovely?" Coralia awaited his response with a beatific smile.

She was so like her mother. It still broke Lindh's heart sometimes to look at her, reminded of the loss of his sweet love's brightness.

Lindh shook himself out of the tarred pit of memories he often found himself trapped in, grateful for his Coralia. She made him happy, made him laugh with only a raised brow, and brought him joy instead of sorrow. And looking at the man before him, it was evident how well she knew her father and his taste. It had never been a secret to his children that he saw no limitations in who he would enjoy.

Happiness came in all kinds of flavors. Lindh had savored them all.

"Yes, he is beautiful, little one." Even he could recognize the heat in his voice. "Hello, Trillian. My name is Lindh Hali."

The surprise glowing on the tiny morsel's face was delightful, warming Lindh's heart. He smiled kindly at the creature and back to his children, apparently proud of themselves. He was surprised they didn't twinkle-finger each other's hands behind the man's back.

Adamaris, taller than his sister, smiled knowingly. He was darker, like Lindh, with heavy curls that fell to his shoulders. His son would make a great father or sire someday. Since Lindh had raised his children as humans, Adamaris becoming a father would make more sense than him giving birth to a merchild. His son was business minded and managed the restaurant's books, playing with numbers now as he had played with his toys when he was a child, which seemed only a short time ago.

"Good. Let's keep him." Adamaris flashed a huge grin and fist-bumped his twin.

The two glanced at him with a smugness he couldn't begin to question. They had done well with their chosen prey.

"Come on, Trillian, the kitchen's this way. Put your bags down and follow me." Coralia dragged their prize into the kitchen, taking two paper bags that appeared heavy with rounded objects bumping against the surfaces. She hung them on a hook beside a sconce filled with bright summer blooms of roses and carnations. "He's hungry, Father. It would help if you made him something to eat. I'll get him a drink."

Her voice trailed off as the doors to the kitchen closed behind them.

Lindh stared, stunned at first, but how surprised could he be? His Coralia was a whirlwind, and the air around her hummed with her energy whenever she blew through.

He turned to Adamaris. "Does she know if he's taken?"

"I don't believe she cares. To her, no ring means he's available. I can't argue with that. We want our father to be happy. We're completely selfish like that." Adamaris smiled up at him and winked.

Their openness was a carbon copy of their mother and made him smile. While a shadow of remembered pain from her loss still touched him, it was no longer the overwhelming wound it once was.

"In the market, huh?" Lindh rubbed his chin thoughtfully.

Adamaris nodded. "Yes, looking at a list, confused and lost."

Of course, that's what would have appealed to Coralia. Ever the empath, she was drawn to helping others.

"Well, that explains it, then. Something in Trillian must have called to her. It's in Coralia's blood to help."

If Coralia was like his Iliona, she was a Nereid, a mermaid who protected others, humans included. Adding his Guardian half helped her to be a strong individual with a mind of her own. But it did nothing to douse her desire to help those she felt were in need. If anything, she was only more determined to right every wrong of any and every person she came across. She would make a great teacher someday.

"Like our mother?" Adamaris asked.

"Exactly like her," Lindh said, listening as Coralia flitted about, ordering Trillian.

"And he *is* beautiful, Father, is he not?" The innocent tone in Adamaris's voice was not to be trusted.

Lindh turned to Adamaris. He knew his son well.

Adamaris's devilish expression left no doubt he was fully aware of how much Trillian had sparked Lindh's interest.

"Not you, too, Adamaris." Lindh sighed, tossing the towel he carried on the bar top before taking a seat. He'd done well picking up bar stools that could hold a man his size. They were comfortable, the leather supple, and encouraged someone to linger. Perfect.

"Yes, Father. Me, too." An earnest look replaced the devilish one. "Coralia's right. We're both in college now, and you're here alone when you could be happy with someone. We saw a possibility and took a chance. You could do the same."

Lindh grunted.

Adamaris moved closer and leaned against Lindh's shoulder. "Trillian could make you happy, Father.".

"I don't know," Lindh whispered, but the possibility fell hard into his soul.

Adamaris crossed his arms. "You don't know what? If you'd like to smile for reasons other than your children or to laugh other than when you're chatting with Batair. You've done nothing but live your life for us. So we think it's past time you have another reason to be happy."

Lindh listened to Coralia as she corralled their guest and the shy murmurs in response that he longed to hear more closely.

"Yes, Coralia and I agree. It's your turn for happiness. Take it," Adamaris insisted.

"Father," Coralia called from within the depths of the kitchen. "You and Adamaris come in here. We're hungry, remember. Be nice to your guest."

Adamaris laughed. "She beckons."

"That she does. Come along, son, or she'll be out here after us." Lindh shrugged.

Adamaris chuckled as he walked away, but the glance he threw back was both unrelenting and unapologetic.

No longer wanting to linger, Lindh rose and followed his son to the kitchen. He felt drawn to the man behind those double doors no matter the hesitancy he'd shown Adamaris.

Lindh hoped his kitchen impressed Trillian. Industrial-sized appliances filled the space, shiny and clean, while his soldiers hustled around, prepping meals and getting them out of the kitchen and onto the guest's tables. He loved colorful light, so when planning the kitchen, he had used stained-glass windows in the exterior walls to bring in the sunlight. And at the large wooden table claiming the center of the room where he and his family could sit and eat in peace was Coralia with Trillian.

Trillian made his dick harder than a brick and his breath harder to take in. Those limpid green eyes the color of sea glass, soft and lost, looked everywhere but at him, and Lindh wanted nothing more than to be the younger man's focus.

Why fight it? I want to see more of this lovely creature waiting to be devoured by my children. I should intervene to keep him safe, at least.

CHAPTER TWO

Trillian, the third son of Mazu, daughter to Neptune, had no idea how he'd ended up here. One moment he'd been standing in a market grasping a sheet of paper with words scrawled on it in Bridget's handwriting. The next thing he knew, two strangers were whisking him away.

Trillian liked the two young ones and got to know them as they traveled from the market. They claimed to be twins but were so different. The girl, Coralia, loved to laugh and seemed wild and open. While the boy, Adamaris, was calm and thoughtful. He wasn't without warmth, but he appeared to hold it closer to his chest.

He looked around the place the twins had brought him, recognizing it as a restaurant. There were rows and rows of various colors, plants of all kinds, and even some from near his home. He'd picked up strands of seaweed and sighed.

Being among the land dwellers was different. There were no dolphins to play with or octopuses to tease. He had found none of his favorite foods here but had enjoyed some of the cooked delicacies he tried. French fries were now his new favorite food. He loved licking the salt from his fingers. They were best when hot and crispy, but he'd sometimes hide a few in his bed for later. Bridget and her sisters warned him that keeping food in his bed invited insects. Unless he wanted to eat bugs, he'd best keep his food in places where it belonged.

He loved the scents surrounding him in this place, especially that of the children's father. The man smelled delicious, like home. He wanted to lick him just like the salt from his fingers. The man appeared human, but something about the guy reminded him of merpeople. It wasn't uncommon for branches of merpeople to reside in the surface world, mixing with humankind. His brother, Batair, lived on land with his mate. Besides, weren't they all one?

He tilted his head and stared at the father. *This man calls to me. Would I be able to taste the ocean on his skin?*

His brothers, Kamau and Batair, both had families—their mates and their young—and were happy. He hadn't given the idea of a mate or family much thought. Despite being one of Neptune's grandsons, he was more focused on himself and his art. He liked his freedom no matter how much he enjoyed visiting with his nephews and nieces. But he saw the love Coralia and Adamaris had for their father, which made him wonder a little about a family.

Trillian listened to Coralia's chatter as he looked around the kitchen. The two urchins who kidnapped him meant well, but he felt he had failed the first of his solo tasks on land. He was supposed to use paper money to buy the items on Bridget's shopping list. It was her way of giving him practice living on the surface.

Bridget was the mother of Aoki, Batair's mate, and a surrogate parent to Kamau. She and her sisters also owned a restaurant where people went for drinks and food and talk. Food was apparently the common denominator for communities, whether in water or on land.

Bridget was a witch, bright and beautiful with a fiery spirit. Trillian was instantly overwhelmed, but she and her sisters, Iona and Cara, quickly warmed him with their kindness. Bridget's hair was bone white, her sister Iona's a bold red, and Cara's a blend of black and gold. Together, they were a force to be reckoned with, complimenting each other in spirit, a portrait waiting to be captured by Trillian's itchy fingers. Art was the reason he was here, after all. He wanted to learn and to paint. He was impatient to develop the talent it would take to do just that.

The sisters had been supportive, helping him find the right school in Charleston and a place to live that wasn't too far from them. Bridget had supported him when he'd insisted on living alone, wanting the whole experience of life as a human adult. Wary, his mother had agreed, but only when Bridget stepped in, saying she would keep a watchful eye.

It had been his mother's idea to stay with the sisters, as she and Bridget were great friends. She wanted her son somewhere she could trust. The two had gained a relationship years before when Bridget took his mother in and cared for her as she had Kamau after that.

He smiled as he recalled his introduction to Bridget.

He stepped onto the surface world beside Mazu, and she immediately called Bridget, who met them at the shore. After hugs and laughter, Mazu looked at him and sighed. He took a hopeful breath.

Bridget smiled at Mazu warmly. "You've no worries, sister of the sea. Lovely Mazu, daughter of Neptune, we will keep Trillian as we did your oldest son Kamau and watch over him as we have your guardian son, now my son-in-law, Batair, who is at home right now in Aoki's care, big with their seventh child, our grandchild. Guardian he is, but he is also my son's treasure and would not be allowed out of their home with Aoki's dragon stomping around protectively. I can barely get near him when he is like this. He is loved as we love you and love Trillian. Your family is our family. We honor that bond. We know Trillian is one of your youngest, and he is special to you."

When Trillian moved closer to Mazu, seeking her touch, she drew him near and rubbed her cheek against his. Her scent, from her cultivated ocean flowers, reminded him of home and safety. Though he was ready to explore, he was slow to leave his mother's arms. And yet, there was more out there for him. He could feel it thrumming through his bones. He shivered with excitement.

"He is my very own, loved greatly, as I love all my children," his

mother said, her voice powerful with affection. "I would not lose him to the surface world."

"I am not asking to stay, Mother. Just to visit," Trillian whispered.

She was protective of all her children, wanting them to be near her. Batair having chosen to remain on the surface made her worry that Trillian would do the same.

Mazu sighed. "Father Neptune has given you a year, not more. He is more worried than me that we will lose you to dry land. You are as special to him as you are to me."

As if to echo her words, the ocean rose and fell about them, crashing wildly against the shore. Trillian bent and touched the water, which climbed around his arm, nearly sucking him in before pushing him forward.

Mazu nodded. "He understands your desire to paint and to sculpt, to have the chance to experience a world unlike your own as I have, as your brothers have. But as I returned to the sea, my love, you will also. Is this understood?"

Thinking nothing of it then, Trillian had promised, and Mazu released him to Bridget, who had taken him into her arms and smiled.

"Welcome, my third son of the sea. You're going to love it here." Bridget laughed and opened her arms to welcome Trillian.

"For a year, Bridget," Mazu warned.

"For a year, sister." Bridget agreed.

And here Trillian was with his first solo task thwarted.

The ringing of the cell phone Bridget had given him was not a surprise, as one of the sisters, usually Cara, the more nurturing of the three, often called to check on him at Bridget's beckoning, no doubt.

Sliding his finger across the glass, he answered, "Hello."

"Hi, youngling. How was shopping?" It was indeed Cara.

Of all the sisters, Cara was his favorite. She was bright and happy, always smiling. While he knew Bridget would keep him safe, it was Cara with whom he felt most welcome. She loved music and shared his joy in art. She'd visited the art school with him and helped him select his classes. It was almost like having a sister on land, while Bridget was more like a mother, watchful and protective. As for Iona, she seemed more comfortable with a weapon in hand. Or that was how he pictured her.

Realizing his mind had wandered, as it often did, he answered Cara's question. "It was fine. I made friends, it would appear. And now, I sit in a restaurant's kitchen waiting."

There was a pause as three voices murmured in the background before Cara spoke into the phone, "You have? You'll have to tell me more."

"Of course, as soon as I return to my dwelling."

"Good. I'll keep the others at bay. They at least want to know where this restaurant is, or I can't promise they won't magically appear." Cara laughed, but there was a thread of seriousness beneath her words.

Looking for anything that might tell him the restaurant's name, he picked up a powder blue napkin with the words *Iliona's Sea Haven* printed in the center. A printer had designed them beautifully, with a mermaid sitting on a rock looking out toward the sea as its logo.

"The place is called *Iliona's Sea Haven*," Trillian said and tried picturing what little he'd seen of the restaurant on the way in but failed. He would have to notice his surroundings better. Instead, his attention had been on the giant man introduced as Coralia and Adamaris's father. And now, he sat at a table in the center of the kitchen, watching as men and women worked harmoniously to create meals for the guests. They chatted, chopped, and sang while others rushed in and out, plates in hand. He loved the flow of it. It was the art of life, of togetherness.

"*Iliona's Sea Haven*," Cara repeated. There was murmuring

again. "We know the place. Good people. Okay, you sit, talk, have fun, and act human-y. Let us know when you get home so we can get the items from the market."

Trillian laughed. "Of course."

He knew the fresh onions, parsley, and sea eggs from the list were a lure to get him home, but he appreciated the care just the same. He lived close enough to the sisters he could walk if he wanted. It was the independence he desired but the watchful eye they wished to keep. It worked. It wasn't as if he would have anything to hide from them.

"Here." Coralia handed him a large glass filled with a yellow drink with bits floating around in a circle.

It was a fruit drink of some sort, he was sure. He was also a little wary, but Coralia's smile was sweet and open, encouraging.

"Try it. My father makes the best lemonade for miles. Not sure what you were going to be doing today, so no alcohol for you. Maybe later, though?" She laughed.

It was her laugh that did it for him. It reminded him of Kamau's laughter, all musical and free.

If I were human, would she capture me as a siren?

It was an exciting thought. Trillian knew nothing about these people or this place, but he wanted to—especially the man outside the doors.

He took a sip and quickly fell in love with the lemonade. It was sharp and tangy. And sweet. He took another sip, trying to compare it to drinks from his home. "This is delicious. I have had nothing like this lemonade. How might I take some with me?"

Pleasure sparkled in Coralia's eyes. "We'll fill a container for you, Trillian. No worries. You won't go home empty-handed. You're our new friend."

He liked that idea. So far, the time he'd spent in the surface world had been enjoyable. He had the sisters, and it seemed he'd made some new friends.

14

When the door to the kitchen opened, Adamaris walked in, followed by the twin's father. Trillian forgot to breathe at the sight of the man, who walked over to a stove and started dishing up something.

The man's tall form easily towered over Trillian. He wore his hair to his shoulders in dark curls, and his skin was tanned as if he had spent hours in the sun. He was rough and muscular, with a shirt that strained to wrap around his biceps, and hips Trillian wanted to grip.

The man carried the plate of whatever it was toward the table. Trillian's mouth went dry with want, so he sipped more lemonade. It would seem there were other things he wished to try in this new world.

"I've brought you something to eat, Trillian. My little ones mentioned you were hungry from your trip to the market."

Lindh. His name is Lindh. Trillian savored the sound of it floating through his mind. He would eat whatever the man chose to share with him.

"Yes, I am hungry," Trillian said. "I would love to try your meal. Would you sit with me?" He wanted Lindh next to him so he could enjoy the man's intoxicating scent.

Lindh's eyes widened, and he licked his lips. "I have to go out and take care of the house."

"Nope, I got that, Dad. Coralia and I will cover while you sit with Trillian," Adamaris said, taking the plate from Lindh's hand and setting it on the table.

"Just what I was thinking, Adamaris." Coralia pulled out a chair across from Trillian and helped settle Lindh in. "You two sit and talk. He's all yours, Dad."

And then they were gone, the background noise fading as Trillian stared at the man sitting across from him.

Lindh coughed. "Subtle, my two."

Trillian smiled. "Subtle?"

Lindh sighed and looked around, his gaze following the

kitchen staff as they moved about purposefully.

Purple. Trillian made a mental note of Lindh's eye color so he could try and capture it later.

"No doubt they're in on it, too." Lindh nodded toward the staff. "Not one has asked me a question since I've been here."

"Because we don't need anything, boss," one of the men answered after dropping off a drink for Lindh. He nodded at Trillian and walked away.

Trillian turned back to Lindh, who looked at him from beneath long lashes, almost shy but charming. Trillian's insides quivered.

"I . . . They . . . My children think I need to make friends and get out more." He stumbled through his words.

Trillian touched Lindh's wrist, hoping to calm him. Lindh smiled, his eyes warming as he gazed at Trillian.

"I would like to be your friend, Lindh." He wanted more than that. This man made him feel confident and bold. Like he needed to take charge, for once.

CHAPTER THREE

L indh's skin heated beneath Trillian's touch, and a thrum of need immediately weaved around him. He took a deep breath, in and out, then picked up the glass and drank from it, appreciating the moment to think.

Trillian was so beautiful, making Lindh's heart beat faster just looking at him. White-blonde hair fell over his shoulders, clasped in a loose ponytail, one Lindh could almost feel his fingers running through. He wore a blue shirt, one tanned shoulder revealed. A few bracelets adorned his slim wrists, but his fingers were strong. Lindh appreciated the strength in the men he chose to take to his bed. Although he rarely had the time, he still had needs.

But something about Trillian called to him, torching him from the inside and sending flames coursing through his veins.

"I don't have many friends here, and it would be nice to have someone to talk to," Trillian explained, taking his hand away.

Lindh almost protested, not wanting to lose Trillian's' touch. Instead, he smiled, hoping Trillian could see the desire he held.

"I have only one friend here, like a brother to me. I could always use another one," Lindh said quietly.

Trillian nodded and sipped his drink, and Lindh watched him swallow. He could think of other things he wanted this beautiful creature to taste. Could Trillian see his hunger? In response, Lindh's cock twitched, stretching his pants, but he did his best to ignore it.

Azizi brought a plate by and set it in front of Trillian. "Fresh bread."

Dorian carried a bowl filled with butter and placed it beside the plate. "Nothing like butter for hot bread."

Next came Edra, who refilled Trillian's glass.

"Thank you. You are all very kind." Trillion's sea glass eyes glanced at each of Lindh's staff and back to Lindh before delicately taking a piece of bread, separating it, buttering it, then choosing a jelly.

Satisfied, Lindh's people nodded and went back to work.

"They are very attentive," Trillian said.

"I would imagine the same thing that draws me to you also draws them." Lindh nodded toward the dish he'd brought for Trillian. "I hope you like the pasta. I mixed bits of clam and oyster inside, favorites of mine."

Trillian smiled. "They are favorites of mine as well. Are you drawn to me, Lindh?" He stared directly at him.

Lindh couldn't look away and took a nervous breath. "I am, Trillian."

"Perhaps, more than friendship then could exist for us?" Trillian's gaze remained focused.

"Perhaps."

Lindh watched as Trillian ate the pasta, twirling it around his fork and savoring each bite. Lindh took another drink, needing the distraction.

"This is delicious, Lindh. Thank you."

"You're welcome. It gives me pleasure to see someone delight in what I've prepared. Especially you. So, tell me about yourself."

Trillian smiled, then took another bite, slowly chewing as if deciding what to say. Lindh waited, his patience infinite where this man was concerned.

"I'm here to study art for a year."

An artist.

Trillian continued eating, taking time to enjoy each morsel. Lindh enjoyed watching him. He could see Trillian as an artist. With those long fingers, he could draw, paint, or sculpt. There were shells in his hair, reminiscent of Lindh's people. The bracelets were thin, with pieces of colored stone decorating them, catching the light in the room as he lifted the fork to his mouth.

"A year? Surely studying art would take longer than that. Several?" He hoped he would have more time to know this man. Unfortunately, a year would be too short.

"Yes, but I have come to focus on specific styles, capture those skills, and add to my own. The university promised I could take courses of interest without selecting a major." Trillian set his fork down and used his napkin to dab at his pretty lips.

Lindh would have licked them clean, but instead, he asked, "Would you like more?"

"No, this was enough. I appreciate your kindness." Trillian looked at the door. "Your children?"

"Oh, the twins. They're out taking care of the restaurant for me. I don't usually take the time to sit. I'm typically out there, operating my place."

"Ah, I've taken you away from your responsibilities." Trillian nodded, moving to stand.

"No. I wanted to sit and talk with you. Please stay a moment."

Trillian hesitated, scrutinizing him. "Are you certain?"

"I've never been more certain of anything in my life."

Lindh's earnest expression must have convinced Trillian, because he settled in the seat once again. "Tell me what interests you about art, and why only a year?"

Trillian appeared thoughtful, his gaze elsewhere, beyond the kitchen walls', perhaps even the restaurant itself.

"I have a different life than most with my responsibilities

as a member of my family. To visit here required special permission from our patriarch. As such, I was given a year." His gaze returned to Lindh. "But that's fine. A year is a long time. Days. Weeks. Months. If I fill that time with pearls of knowledge, I will have a wealth of information to take home. I have practiced independently, but would like to work with experts and receive training."

"I hope you will give yourself grace, Trillian. Any skill takes time to perfect."

"Yes, but I would like a foundation and techniques. That is all I require. Then I will return home as agreed." His smile was soft as if remembering happy times at home.

Lindh remembered a home from ages past, one that had failed him and the woman he loved. In the end, there had been no tender smiles for them, no joy—only pain and betrayal from people he trusted.

"What was that look for," Trillian asked with concern, placing his hand over Lindh's.

"Nothing. You just looked so happy when you thought of going back. It made me think of my own home and how there is nothing for me there," Lindh said.

Trillian lifted Lindh's hand and kissed it. "I'm sorry, Lindh. I would only have you happy."

A thrill course through Lindh at having his hand held gently by Trillian, his skin warm from the kiss of the lips he craved.

"You have such a kind heart, Trillian. I am sure your loved ones miss you. I would certainly miss you." Lindh could easily have removed his hand from Trillian's hold, but he enjoyed it there. The thrum of energy was welcome, unusual. He didn't want it to end.

"I am, but I have family here as well, a brother."

"A brother?"

"Yes, he also came to visit, but he remained. It worries my

family that I might make the same decision. But I gave my word, and they know I will keep it." Trillian smiled. "While I look forward to this experience and new friends, my home is where my heart is."

Lindh nodded. "Perhaps, but then you haven't begun to experience here or your new friends." Lindh turned his hand until he'd captured Trillian's fingers, holding them.

"I haven't, but I look forward to doing so."

Lindh shivered from the heat in Trillian's eyes.

They chatted longer about Trillian's excitement over the school he would attend. Lindh didn't know much about the place, but the way Trillian's eyes lit up when he talked about what he hoped to learn there made him happy. He wanted the chance to hear more. He wanted to be a part of Trillian's joy and see life through his eyes.

Lindh nodded to Azizi, who carried a packed to-go carton and bag. He dropped the package on the table, grinning at Lindh before walking out of the kitchen.

He shook his head and sighed. "It is late, and I would like to take you home." He wasn't ready to part from Trillian.

Trillian looked around and seemed to notice that they were alone now. Nodding, he said, "I would like that."

CHAPTER FOUR

Trillian's belly jittered and danced like a jellyfish bloom as he waited for Lindh while he spoke to his son and daughter. Coralia glowed as if she'd won a prize, but Trillian felt like he had captured the trophy. Adamaris nodded, then reached inside his pocket and pulled out a small shiny square. Lindh protested, and Adamaris returned the packet to his pocket, but his grin was wicked with humor.

"You should take it," Adamaris' whispered.

The boy probably thought Trillian couldn't hear him, but he could and listened to their conversation with interest.

"While I thank you for your care, son, I have no need for it. We're not going to do anything. I'm just taking him home."

Coralia piped in, "You say that now, but neither of us would blame you if you did. In fact, we would cheer for you." She laughed.

Trillian was struck again by how like a siren her laugh was. He was curious to hear what it would sound like for her to sing.

"Et tu, Brute?" Lindh glared at his daughter.

"Oh, heck no. You did not just quote words from Caesar to me," Coralia said.

"Well, as a future history teacher, I thought it apt. Now, are you certain about closing for the night? Of course, my people will be here to ensure all is well, but you don't usually close."

Adamaris huffed. "We have this, Father. And we trust your soldiers to assist us. Coralia and I must study, so we'll close up shop and head straight home." Adamaris raised his hand with three fingers in the air, thumb and little finger touching. "Scout's honor."

Lindh sighed but then glanced over to where Trillian stood and smiled.

Trillian smiled back, waiting patiently.

Adamaris laughed, but there was nothing siren-like about his laugh. Instead, it was deep and silky and probably earned him many first and second glances.

The boy smirked. "Sure you don't want it?"

"You know, you're not too old to be put on punishment, urchin." Lindh glared but pulled Adamaris to him for a hug and kissed him on the temple. "You know I worry."

It was Coralia's turn next for hugs and kisses, and Trillian's heart warmed at how much Lindh loved his children. He reminded himself once again that he didn't want children. He enjoyed watching young everywhere, swimming, playing, and getting into all kinds of mayhem. And he was a doting uncle to his nieces and nephews, but a father? No, not for him. Still, he liked seeing Lindh's eyes shine with love for his twins.

"We know, Father. But someday, we'll leave the nest, and it would be best if you weren't alone. You need someone." Coralia smiled, then glanced at Trillian.

It was Lindh's turn to laugh this time, and the sound vibrated through Trillian's body, traveling down to the tip of his cock, making it drip with need. Trillian breathed deeply, working to control himself. He would not take Lindh tonight.

But he would take him.

People often assumed that because Trillian was slight in stature, he was not powerful in his own right. He was, and he'd proven himself many times. As a man of Neptune, it was his duty to be prepared to fight at any time, Guardian or not. He'd trained like every other member of his family.

He relished taking charge, commanding. He loved seeing

a man on his knees. He loved caring for them and hearing them scream.

He burned to hear Lindh scream his name.

But not now. Trillian could wait. So he watched while Lindh readied himself, calling him when it was time to go.

Trillian liked the feel of riding with the windows down, the wind whipping at his hair. He admired the look of Lindh's hands as they gripped the wheel, his brown fingers long and thick. Like the man.

He glanced at Lindh's profile.

Adamaris had called the men working with Lindh his soldiers. He said the words with sincerity, meaning Lindh had served in the military. Trillian wasn't familiar with the warriors of the surface dwellers, but he could see Lindh as a Guardian. Tall, muscular, and constantly aware. He scanned the drive ahead as a Guardian would search for danger.

As a man of Neptune, Trillian was familiar with the traits. Batair and his brother Orin did the same, both Guardians. It was an innate ability to protect others at the cost of their own lives if necessary.

Trillian had' fought to come ashore alone and had made Batair promise to keep his distance, insisting he could protect himself. Although he chose to use his hands to craft and create, he could also use them as weapons. His ability to send out blasts of energy from his fingertips had not left him when he emerged from the sea.

Or course, I tested it. I had to prove I wouldn't need the contingent of Guardians that my mother had brought with us.

As one of Mazu's youngest, Trillian understood her desire to protect him, but he could fair well on his own.

"You are not far from Sister's Three," Lindh said, turning on the road that would take them to Trillian's cottage. It was a small dwelling, just enough for one.

"I love it there. The women are kind, and my mother entrusted them with my care. I've had many opportunities to enjoy delicious meals I've never had. They are artists in their own right." Trillian's expression filled with warmth.

Lindh loved the look, but something about Trillian's words drew his attention.

Odd words for one beyond the age of maturity.

But then there were several statements the beautiful creature mentioned that attracted Lindh's ardor . . . and curiosity.

"Entrusted them with your care?" he asked.

"Yes, my mother and the Sisters Three's owners are close, family almost. So when I asked for permission to learn here, I was trusted only within their care. It was difficult for my mother and our patriarch to let me come as my brothers had visited, and one did not return. But he fell in love."

Lindh pulled into the home's driveway, his tires grinding on the sandy path. "Surely, she would not fault her son for finding love."

Trillian gently shook his head. "No, she would not. Our patriarch, my grandfather, however, was not pleased.

"My brother's place was with our people, and as my mother chose between her love and our people so many years ago, his choice should have been easy to make."

Trillian's tone of finality was challenging for Lindh to accept. Someone so young should not remain trapped in antiquated ideas and moors.

"I think you have never been in love, Trillian, or you would truly know how difficult such a decision is."

Trillian' smiled softly. "No, I can't say I've ever been in love, but I know what my word means. I know what promises are and what roles mean for my home."

"There may come a day, young prince, when your old promises will mean nothing compared to your heart."

Trillian looked at him, seeming befuddled. "Young

prince?"

Lindh loved the color of Trillian's eyes. Earlier, he'd compared them to sea glass. Now, they were a brilliant green that shone in the moonlight, nearly glowing. He found himself once again trapped with his gaze.

"There's something about you, the way you speak and hold yourself, that reminds me of royalty. And then there's that distance, that bit of innocence that appeals to me."

Trillian laughed. "I'm no innocent, Lindh. I have been with men before."

His eyes twinkled with his laughter, but Lindh wanted to see them sparkle for an entirely different reason. One that involved slick skin and gripping hands.

Lindh chuckled. "Trillian, there is more to innocence than having one's body known by another. With such an alluring form as yours, I would be surprised if men and women did not simply fall at your feet, eager to have a taste of you."

Trillian's gaze trailed to Lindh's lap and back to his face. "Even you?"

Lindh' laughed huskily this time. "Even me, Trillian? Especially me. The very moment I laid my gaze upon you, I wanted you. Have no doubt. But I find myself wanting more than to taste you. I would like to know you."

Trillian unclicked his seatbelt and started to crawl over the console, but Lindh stopped him with a touch to his wrist.

"No, Trillian."

Trillian moved back, his surprise clear. "I wish to taste your lips, Lindh."

Lindh hummed. "If you kiss me, I don't know if I'll be able to stop at just a kiss. The very scent of you, your touch, burns through my flesh to my very soul. I've never felt this way, and I need to know more about you before I lose control." He'd held on to his control for years. As a guardian, as a husband, as a father, as a widow, and as a restaurateur. His control was a tool of survival for him. He couldn't lose that now when it truly mattered so much.

Trillian's pout was cute, so sweet. Lindh wanted to feel it against his lips and dip his tongue inside to sample its heat. But he wanted more than entry into Trillian's body. Instead, he reached out and touched his hand, the skin soft against his fingertips.

"Tell me about your home. About you. Listening to you speak of a home makes me wonder about the one I left behind." How many years had Lindh tried to wipe away the memories of his past? His childhood? His friendships? When he'd left the world he'd grown up in, the one that had ultimately betrayed him, Lindh had struggled to make a new life on the surface world. Unlike Trillian, he'd made no such promises to return. Instead, he promised to love his twins without fail and ensure they grew up safe and happy.

He'd given his children everything he felt Iliona would have wanted. But had he forgotten his happiness? Failed to live as both Coralia and Adamaris said he had? Had his remaining alone for so many years broken his promise to them instead?

At the moment, all Lindh could think of was the pleasure of being next to Trillian. He smelled of the ocean and sunshine. He was bright and sweet yet carried himself with a strength Lindh admired.

The way Trillian seemed to quietly command those around him from the moment he'd sat at Lindh's kitchen table made Lindh want to experience that control. He was a big man, towering over most. And often, when he took a lover, he performed in the role expected of him.

Dominate. Control. Demand. Conquer.

But that wasn't Lindh.

He needed . . . no, he thrived on being cared for, tended to, and loved on. He ached for a lover to take over, to control him.

He had tried a few times to reveal his desires, but they had never been fulfilled. So instead, he'd fucked them and achieved less-than-pleasing orgasms. And he'd let it go.

Yet he sensed the thread of power in Trillian. He craved it but refused to light a match whose fire would extinguish in seconds. No, he wanted the flames he felt with Trillian to flourish . . . for both of them.

He needed to know more about Trillian.

The man in question looked at the cottage and then back to him. "Would you like to come inside, Lindh?"

Lindh swallowed weakly at hearing the heat in Trillian's voice. "I would, but I can't. Please allow me to watch you enter. It's my calling to ensure safety and protection."

Trillian smiled but moved to exit the car.

"Wait. I want to take you on a train ride," Lindh rushed to say.

Trillian's eyes widened. "A train ride?"

"Yes, it was one of the things I loved when I arrived here years ago. My twins always enjoyed it. Share it with me?" He hoped Trillian would say yes. He wanted to spend time with him. But not alone until he could hold himself back from not begging to be fucked by Trillian. And he knew, without a doubt, he would.

Trillian nodded. "That sounds nice. I've never been on a train ride. Should I wear something specific?"

"As you are now is pleasing, beautiful Trillian. May I pick you up at twelve tomorrow? Sundays are when I take time away from the restaurant. I'd love to spend the day with you."

"Yes. Yes, I would like that, too." Trillian nodded, exiting the car and pulling his bag from the back seat. Once more, he glanced at Lindh. "Are you sure I can't convince you to enter my home?"

Trillian's warm voice washed over him, making the offer much more enticing. And while Lindh felt a wave of something hit him, he gripped the steering wheel and remained strong.

"You could convince me to do anything your heart desires. I only ask that you give me the time to be ready."

Trillian nodded. "You are delightful, Lindh. Goodnight."

He watched as Trillian entered his home, closing the door behind him. When a light indicated Trillian was safe and settling in, he breathed easier.

Until tomorrow . . .

CHAPTER FIVE

Trillian watched from the window as Lindh's car's tail-lights faded into darkness.

He had hoped the night would end differently, with him seated between Lindh's round cheeks, plunging inside his luscious hole. So few didn't want what he offered. But Lindh appealed to him in such a way that he couldn't resist at least trying.

A year spent with Lindh, taking and giving what they both clearly wanted, would have been a perfect accompaniment to learning the skills he dreamed of.

He messaged Cara, choosing to drop off the grocery items the next day instead. Cara sent him a heart and a smile in response.

Then he felt a call from home. He wasn't surprised to feel Graham on the other end, knowing Kamau would have his mate do his dirty work to check on his younger sibling. Kamau knew Trillian would never reject a call from Graham.

The family all loved Graham, who surrounded himself with his and Kamau's many sons and daughters. Which wasn't an impossible feat, as Kamau kept his mate in a constant state of propagation.

He reached up and opened the circle of communication in the air that arced with a spin of electricity. He smiled even now, as Graham came into view through the portal, he could see Graham's rounded belly. It was well pronounced with what his family knew Graham was hoping would be another girl. Boys and only one girl, Shahena, filled their family.

Shahena needed a sister, someone to play with as she grew, rather than the army of brothers who would potentially run off any suitor or drive her to madness as brothers often did.

Graham waved from his rocking chair, bouncing a little babe against his chest. His hair had lost its bristly cut years ago. Long strands of silver now danced among the darker-colored length.' He was clearly happy with the joys of parenthood, while the very idea filled Trillian with unease.

Who knew when Kamau lived on the surface world, he would find his mate while working with his father, a religious leader, and their mother's mate? The way Kamau told it, he'd spotted Graham immediately and waited for his chance at love. As for Graham, he said he fell into Kamau's musical trap and never wanted to leave. As Kamau was a siren, Trillian tended to side with Graham.

"Well, Trillian, entertain me with tales of your first day without your mother there," Graham announced.

His mother had finally gone home the day before, secure with his word to return home. He suspected she'd enjoyed her time, though, sneaking off to see her mate if the darkened shadows at her neck and shoulders were a hint to her nefarious activities.

How many lovers had his mother enjoyed since she'd left her mate until Trillian's brothers and sisters abounded? Many, but none of them had lasted, even if said mate was unworthy of her love. Nonetheless, they were all tied to the surface world because of a mate she couldn't leave behind.

'Life was better lived knowing the boundaries one possessed and not submitting their control to mercurial emotions. Needs could be satisfied elsewhere. Family, home, and one's word were everything. Those were the only things that made sense.

"I've made a friend." Trillian smiled, fully aware he should have kept that information to himself. But he was too excited, too eager to share.

Why not share with Graham?

His human brother was everyone's confidant and was known for harboring secrets, particularly with him not being under Father Neptune's rule, sire to merchildren or not.

Graham smiled, his brown eyes sparkling with mischief. "You did? Don't want your siblings hearing of this, do you?" He cocked his head thoughtfully. "What's it worth to you?"

Trillian laughed. "If you want another necklace, spoiled love of my brother, all you have to do is ask."

"But this is so much more fun." Graham chuckled. "And you know how much I love your work."

Trillian did and would give the man anything he asked. After all, Graham's encouragement to learn more was what had prompted him to seek permission to visit the surface world where he could study the skills he desired firsthand. As a former human soldier, Graham had seen the world. His stories of the art in cities and countries he'd visited were priceless.

In return, Trillian had gifted him with jewelry he'd made from natural stones and fossils from the ocean world. Many valued his pieces, but for Graham, he'd made special ones that included the colors and shapes from stories he'd shared.

But Trillian needed more. More mediums. More styles. He wanted to paint and sculpt. He craved different shades and hues. He wanted the ability to create with fine detail, recreate pieces he'd only dreamed of when he sat with Graham some evenings.

"You would make me give up every secret," Trillian teased, leaning back against the headboard and pulling up the covers to settle around his legs.

"Well, as my mate will only allow me to travel so far, it's your stories I have to live through now."

Ha! If Graham wanted Trillian to believe him unhappy, he would have to do better than that. He saw the joy on his face when surrounded by his family when Kamau kissed him on his eyelids and held him tight. There was nothing more that Graham wanted.

Trillian told Graham about his day, from his confusion over the items on Bridget's list to his virtual kidnapping by Lindh's beautiful twins.

"And just like that, you went with them?" Concern filled Graham's voice, his military background peeking through no doubt.

When Graham's son, Narin, took the babe from him, the older boy greeted Trillian and left.

"He's growing fast."

"Narin? Yes, he will leave soon to train with the guardians." Graham looked fondly after his son.

"He'll be ready," Trillian said. He had no worries about Narin. From an infant, there had always been something different about him. A blend of human and merman or not, he would prove to be one of the best Guardians the ocean world would ever know.

"He already is. Now, don't try to distract me. Continue."

"As you and my brothers have already insisted, I am well prepared to take care of myself both in the ocean and out. Now . . . You will have to meet these two, Graham. They were eager to take me with them like they'd won a prize. I wanted to see why." It had been their smiles and their sincerity. The moment they'd turned the corner, their gazes had stopped on Trillian and then turned to each other. Without hesitation, they'd approached him, Coralia grasping his hands, a stranger with so much warmth, he could not have resisted if he'd tried.

"Hm." Graham nodded, apparently still not convinced of Trillian's safety. "And did you like where you ended up?"

Trillian thought of Lindh with his dark curls, broad shoulders, quiet deep voice, and shy smile. "Yes."

"Oh, I've seen that look before. Who is he? Is he the friend you mentioned earlier?"

Narin returned with the twins, Aidan and Nadia, handing each carefully to Graham. Narin was fierce and tender, admirable traits of both parents that should make them proud. His entry into the world had been challenging, but he'd fought and survived.

Narin's laugh when Graham teased him made Trillian grin, their happiness hard to resist. He helped Graham have a drink and shared some food, possibly marlin, one of Graham's favorites. When he finished caring for his siblings and his father, he left with a wave.

Leaning back, Graham soothed the little ones, who settled quickly.

"His name is Lindh, and he's the owner of the restaurant the twins brought me to." Trillian described the food he'd eaten.

"Ah. And Sisters Three did not keep you well enough?"

Trillian laughed. "Well, I had no idea how hungry I was until I laid eyes on such a magnificent banquet of flesh."

They spoke of the next day, a chance to ride on a train, of Trillian taking a sketch pad to capture ideas for future pieces. As they talked, Graham rotated through little ones and then the older children until it was just him and Narin. Knowing this was the time Graham made for his oldest, Trillian moved to close the circle.

"Be good, Trillian, and have fun but with care. And should you want something more, don't be afraid to allow yourself to have it."

"Thank you, Graham. Perhaps." Bidding his brother's mate and Narin goodnight, he closed the circle.

Something more? Did Trillian want that?

Certainly not having what he'd wanted that night, Lindh in his bed, made him want even more. But was there the possibility of something more than physical?

He touched his fingers to his lips, fingers that had been singed when he'd touched Lindh the first time and yet was compelled to do it again later.

No, he wouldn't think about that. He had come here with a purpose. He would not be derailed by cock or by heart.

CHAPTER SIX

Lindh's day started with music, a soundtrack of notes from an electric guitar combined with a lead singer's voice.

He often started his Sundays, his only day off, freeing his home from clutter. As a restaurant owner, he was busy. As a father, life was a whirlwind. But when had he finally realized that his children were now on their own, leaving him behind?

He'd done his job. He'd raised the twins just as his beautiful Iliona would have wanted, making sure they had the best he had to give. He was their protector, their supporter, loving them more than life itself. But they were both grown now, each with a life of their own.

He'd come a long way from the dwelling he'd shared beneath the surface. He had four bedrooms to himself now that his children were no longer around. He typically ate at the restaurant or brought meals from work home, so he didn't have to worry about a messy kitchen. A wipe here or there, and it was gleaming. He was free of squabbles from his children, loud music coming from their bedrooms, mishaps leading to a missed bus or quarreling, and tears over broken hearts he needed to help mend. He had to admit he'd missed the moments when his children needed him most.

He'd occasionally allowed himself a lover but never in his house where the scents of sex would remain. No, the entire home was his and his alone. And while Coralia and Adamaris often dropped by, he'd missed having someone else around. Someone who would look forward to seeing him. Someone to hold at night.

Is it wrong to wish that someone to hold at night could be Trillian?

Lindh had done his best by his family, forsaking any lasting opportunities. He'd remained focused on his children and making sure he provided for them. It meant ensuring the restaurant, purchased using golden coins when he arrived on the surface world, thrived. It was a means of assuring the Guardians, who had left their own lives behind and followed him, had not done so in vain. The restaurant and the home he maintained were a haven for all he considered family.

He'd never found anyone to love after Iliona.

But was I genuinely looking? No.

For so long, his heart had remained broken, the place he'd kept sacred for his mate sheltered. He'd had sex, had never denied himself that. It was easy to share his body. When he'd served as a Guardian, his body had never been his own. But his soul, that which made him who he was, he kept for Iliona alone.

And yet, when he'd seen Trillian, he realized that the constant ache he'd felt for years didn't carry the same weight. Instead, he felt himself open, like a sea anemone with its beautiful tentacles searching. He wanted to draw Trillian to him. Leaving him the night before had been difficult. The urge to accept Trillian's invitation into his home fed his desire to strip the man naked and savor every inch of his golden skin. He craved hearing Trillian cry his name as he tasted him, seeing him fall back against a bed replete.

But he didn't want to stop there. He wanted to take his time, wanted to know him. So he'd asked him to share a train ride.

He'd pulled the train ride entirely out of his hat. It was an experience he'd enjoyed with Coralia and Adamaris and wanted to share with Trillian. He wanted to see him smile and see if anything they saw would inspire the artist in him to create. And while he wished for Trillian's hands on his body, he thought more of capturing his heart.

Though his thoughts were lost in the music as he cleaned, his awareness as a Guardian ensured he didn't miss the knock on his front door.

Lindh dropped the dust cloth on the coffee table in front of his extended sofa, striding to answer.

When he opened the door, he faced a bright and smiling Batair. Seeing the big, bald man grinning ear to ear was almost scary. Some might look at Batair's size and miss his gentleness, kindness, and the way he sought to nurture others. He was tall, wide, and built to create order in a world of chaos. But more often than not, he could be seen braiding his daughter's hair before showing her how to handle a weapon or playing cars with his son after they worked in the garden. Pregnant with his seventh child, he was a cooking dynamo and believed feeding and caring for Lindh was an excellent pastime.

"'Lo there, Lindh. I've been trying my hand at cooking a different recipe."

Lindh glanced at the covered dish Batair held, and his stomach rumbled. He was hungry, and it would be hours before he shared a meal with Trillian. And even then, he feared he might be too nervous to enjoy any food while thinking of another hunger only Trillian could sate.

"Watching a video on a platform created to make a person laugh is not the way to learn to cook." How many videos had Batair sent him, insisting each one was better than the next?

"So I'm a little addicted to watching an app that makes life better, one video clip at a time. Slay me. The cooking videos I've found are fun and easy enough to provide a meal for my family. You can benefit from them, too. Besides, Aoki likes the results." Batair strolled inside, heading to the kitchen.

"Does he, or does he just like anything that you do? You are his mate, after all." Lindh followed Batair, focusing on the dish he carried.

Is that what Lindh thought about now? Having a mate, no longer lonely . . .

Do I want that? Should I try again?

Lindh felt an ache inside when he thought about Trillian—his smile, his gentle touch. He wanted more of that. He wanted to know Trillian and needed more of him, but he wouldn't confuse his desires with wanting a mate.

"What's that smile for, Lindh?" Batair lifted the lid and stirred the pot, and the aroma smelled delicious.

Lindh purposefully ignored Batair's question. "I didn't say I was eating that stuff."

"It won't kill you to try. I want to test this out and see if you like it." Batair looked up and winked at him.

"Or you're just trying to take care of me as you do your children."

Batair raised a brow. "I'm nesting, so it could be possible. I mean, your children are older and rarely here. You work all day at the restaurant and come home just to sleep. The only free time you have is during the weekend, and you use that to clean. Forgive me if I think that you could use a meal and care. And with a seventh child on the way, I want to spread the love. You're also the only person Aoki feels comfortable allowing me to dote on."

Lindh sighed. "Forgive me, Batair. I am hungry and would love to try this interesting dish." There, he hoped he sounded appropriately contrite.

Batair set about preparing the meal. He was familiar with the kitchen and knew where to get the plates and cutlery. He was a nurturer, so Lindh let him nurture him while he finished cleaning.

"Good. Now, speaking of smiles and reasons why," Batair said.

"O ho, now. The true reason for your visit. Have my children been playing spy for you?"

"No, not really. I may have received a message out of the blue from one and then the other, both concerned about their father making a good impression. Less old man and more sexy daddy, something to do with that thick hair you tend to keep in a queue. Whatever that means."

"It means though I'm older, they don't want me seeming decrepit."

Batair smiled. "Kids."

Lindh nodded. "Especially the adult kind."

"Not yet there."

"No, but you will be one day, and it is an endless path of them trying to parent you."

"Yes, well." Batair set a dish on the table. "Come try this."

Lindh tossed the cleaning rag he was using into a bin. After he washed his hands, he sat down and picked up a spoon. Then, with Batair's gaze on him, he opened his mouth and let the broth filled with the savory protein touch his tongue.

Ah, this is good.

Batair quirked his lips. "You like it."

Lindh nodded and enjoyed another heaping spoonful. "Well done, Batair. Quite nice."

"Do I get a handshake?" Batair held out his hand.

They both laughed at Batair's reference to their favorite cooking show where Paul Hollywood would shake the hand of the baking contestant stunning enough to please his distinguished palate.

"Handshake it is," Lindh said with a sweep of his hand, which Batair accepted like it was his honor.

Batair smiled happily, prepared a bowl for himself, and picked up a roll.

Lindh reached out and said, "I'll take one of those. Blue?"

"I like traditional Hawaiian bread, so I figured why not."

Lindh bit into the roll, then coughed and pointed at the water next to him. "You're going to need some of that."

"Okay, a few things to work on."

"No harm done. I appreciate your bringing me a meal."

Batair nodded, digging into his bowl with his roll, then waving it at Lindh. "Use it in the broth," he advised.

Lindh dunked the bread into the meaty broth. Humming, he agreed with Batair. It was a great accompaniment to the dish. "I like this."

"I knew you would. Reminded me of home."

"That it does."

Batair's eyes widened. "Not as much pain in those words, my friend."

Lindh nodded. "Perhaps it's time to move on. Let go."

Batair leaned back fully, placing his hand on his rounded belly, and stared at him. "I never thought I would hear those words from you."

Could meeting Trillian and spending time with him for such a short period have had that much of an effect on me?

He liked the thought of that possibility and realized he had lost the anger and grief he'd held onto for many years.

"Neither did I." Lindh finished eating.

Batair watched him searchingly. "Okay. First, let me say that I hope my own young will love me as much as yours do you. Coralia and Adamaris only want your happiness, and with your statement, it sounds like their wishes may become a possibility."

Lindh was the first to admit how lucky he was. Raising his twins as a lone parent had not been easy. He hadn't expected it to be. He poured all his love for his wife into each day with them. It had paid off.

And now?

Maybe there was a second chance at happiness for himself.

"I love the twins. They're good kids," Lindh said.

"Good adults ready to see their father cared for and happy," Batair corrected.

Lindh finished with the bowl and pushed it aside. "That was very good, Batair. Filling, too."

Batair grinned, "Good enough for your precious list of entrees?"

Lindh placed an index finger against his chin and pondered the idea. "Well, you know how protective I am of my special list of precious entrees. But, still, your meal would certainly fit among them."

"Is that true? And look at me finding a simple recipe from an app." Batair laughed. "Now tell me, what has my nephew and niece so excited? And from how you're changing color, I would say you as well."

"It's nothing important," Lindh said. "I met someone, and he and I will be going on a train ride today."

"A train ride, you say?"

"Yes, what's wrong with that?" Lindh didn't care for the questioning uptick thing in Batair's tone.

"While it may be romantic to you, it may very well be what your daughter and son believe makes you an old man."

"Well, they have their opinions, and I have mine. However, I rather like the idea." Lindh reached for the dish again. "A second bowl, please."

"Really? Now that's a compliment." Batair rose, refilling the bowl. "Now, if you like train rides, that's all that matters. Tell me more."

"Are you living vicariously now, Batair?" Lindh asked before filling his spoon.

"Perhaps a little. Your life seems to be very interesting right now."

"Oh, that's what I am to you. Entertainment." Lindh laughed.

"Not exactly," Batair said before settling back again.

"Then what exactly?"

"I think it's nice that your family is getting you out there. And you, taking a chance to meet someone who might be a person with whom you could share a future. I like it."

Lindh sighed. "I did that years ago."

"I know, my brother, but now is a different time. This is a chance for you to be happy again. The light I already see about you tells me it may be worth our time." Batair tapped the table in emphasis.

"Our time?"

"Yes, you are entertainment, after all. So, it should never be boring."

Lindh laughed loud and hardy, feeling it in the pit of his belly. "Well, he's beautiful. He is like the moon with its silvery light touching the ocean. He glows as if he flows from its depths." Lindh remembered how the light shone on Trillian, unable to forget his brightness.

"Ah, poetry," Batair said. "You have it bad, and you've only known him a day."

"Hours, my friend. I've only known him for hours, but my soul feels as if it were a lifetime. The moment I saw him, I was stunned into stillness."

"Huh. It sounds like the feeling of the earth moving when I met Aoki."

Lindh nodded. "Exactly that."

"And so, this man who captured your breath, you invite him for a train ride. Was this your romantic endeavor?"

"To be honest, it was the first thought. He's an artist. It gives him time to experience a meal with me and scenery to consider for a future project. We can be together but cannot seek each other's heat."

Knowing eyes warmed. "Eager to have him are you?"

"Absolutely. However, I must provide a limit, or I will submit myself to him. I want time with him."

Batair nodded. He knew of Lindh's needs. He had his own. They had spoken of it at length.

"And this person, what's he like? Although, I know how it is to feel the call of a mate."

Lindh took a deep breath, expecting the pain that generally accompanied his thought of a mate, someone to love in place of his Iliona. But he wasn't replacing her. Never would. He would love Iliona forever. It had taken him years to understand this, and he finally believed he'd reached a point where he was ready for a second chance at happiness.

And now, he burned with the desire to have that chance with Trillian, who planned to leave in a year. A year? A lot could happen in so short a time.

Opportunities. Moments. Laughter.

Breakfast after warm nights spent in each other's arms. Sharing joys, tender kisses, heated touches . . . Lindh wanted all of that and more with Trillian.

A year could give him the time he needed to prove his worth.

"What's this look, Lindh?"

Lindh took a drink, savoring it with how dry his throat had become. "He's only here for a year."

"A year? Why?" Batair questioned as he stood to tidy up.

"He's been given a year, he says, and then he returns home."

Batair nodded. "Sounds like home to me. I wonder if he has his own Father Neptune issuing mandates and permissions."

Lindh laughed, but a nervousness ran along his spine. He still feared even saying the name of the god, so he took his bowl to the sink for something to do. "Only you could say that name without an ounce of fear."

"What? Do you think simply whispering my grandfather's name will make him appear?"

"One never knows, and I would choose not to be his target or draw his eye after so many years. I have been on my own. Safe."

"Lindh, you have never been alone, no matter what you think. You may not wear the title of Guardian, but you always belong to the king of the sea."

Lindh looked out of his kitchen window to the gardens beyond. Here, he was free. He followed no Atlantean laws here. Answered no one other than his children. He didn't want to think about this anymore. Instead, he tried to focus on the beautiful young man he would share time with today. That was his here and now—no room for the past.

Batair wisely chose to change the subject. "Now, let's try dessert while you show me what you plan to wear. No old men's clothes, as I promised to my niece and nephew."

Lindh laughed and turned to accept his friend's help.

CHAPTER SEVEN

What does a human wear for a first outing?

Trillian stood in front of the long mirror in the bedroom, the light from the sun peeking through the thin slits in the blinds. It was nice having a home to himself, a space of his own. As one of the youngest of his family, there was always someone around visiting or checking in. And while he loved them and celebrated their closeness, he enjoyed the solitary life he'd begun here.

There were no long looks, no questions of how he fit in or what role he would play as a man of Neptune. Here he was merely a student visiting from another city, a tourist of sorts.

He slid items of clothing from one place to another, determining which would entice Lindh. At home, he would have some idea of what to wear. Typically very little, though he did favor a small swath of fabric now and then to accent his long frame. Here, people felt a need for clothing, as if embarrassed by the body they'd received. Humans.

Only one human demanded his interest that he wanted to please. Lindh was different from what he had expected when the twins pulled him from the market—a work of art. Tall and divine, with golden skin he wanted to taste, and unusual purple eyes. And yet, Lindh already said he wanted to get to know more about him first, as if their being together sexually would distract him. Why did sex have to be such a vast distractor? It was taking and giving . . . a physical expression. Why could it not be the way to get to know each other?

Trillian pictured Lindh. First, he wanted to twine his legs

around Lindh's larger frame and feed his dick into the man's ass. Second? He surprisingly hoped to make Lindh his.

He shook off the thoughts and cast other outfits to the side. He narrowed his search down to three that might at least encourage Lindh's hands to explore Trillian's skin. He'd sensed Lindh wanted him. He just needed a little push.

Later, Trillian waited, sitting in his front room and turning pages in one of the texts he had for class. Still life. Lighting. He got excited at seeing how much he would learn.

He set the book aside when the bell rang and went to the door. The heat in Lindh's eyes was all the confirmation he needed that he'd picked the right outfit. He pulled the man gently inside, enjoying how those purple eyes roamed his body.

"You look far too captivating for a train ride," Lindh whispered and licked his lips.

"Do I? I dressed with you in mind. I hope it satisfies." Trillian smiled, knowing it would appear predatory.

"Greatly. You are dangerous. More so than my twins realized."

Trillian nodded. "I know what I want." He turned to pick up his bag. "I decided to bring some supplies. Art supplies. Never know what I may see out there."

Lindh nodded, then shook his head as if gathering his wits about him.

"I would like a kiss before we go," Trillian said.

"I can't. The moment I touch you, I wouldn't be able to control myself. Your skin is glowing, and your round ass in those tight-as-fuck pants is killing me. My dick is so hard it could chisel granite." Lindh moved away from him cautiously.

Trillian followed him, step for step, making his intentions clear. "A small kiss, Lindh. I'll be gentle." He reached up and took Lindh by the neck and drew him down.

He slammed Lindh's back against the door and took what he wanted, drinking in the taste of Lindh's lips, savoring his mouth and the delicious heat he found there. He delighted in Lindh's deep breaths as he claimed him.

Trillian hummed when Lindh wrapped his hands around his waist, pulling him closer. Opening his eyes, he smiled at Lindh's swollen lips and tousled hair from his fingers. Lindh's chest rose and fell as if he'd run a race.

"Good. That was so good. Thank you, Lindh."

Lindh shivered. "Y-You're welcome, Trillian."

Trillian took the lead, grasping Lindh's hand and drawing him outdoors. "Now, take me to the train. I'd like to see life through your eyes."

As they traveled to the small city of Winnsboro, SC, Lindh told him about his family, owning the restaurant, and places he loved visiting when he had a chance to take time away.

Trillian smiled, adding a question here and there, enjoying the shy heated looks Lindh cast his way. The sheer ivory-colored top he'd chosen with a rose camisole beneath it might have had something to do with that. He'd paired the items with slim-fitting purple pants and thong sandals to complete his look. He kept himself open to Lindh's glances, inviting a touch if Lindh chose to bless him with one.

He'd already kissed Lindh, and now he was eager to have more of him.

"What are you thinking about?" Lindh asked.

"Your life before Charleston." Though it wasn't his immediate thought, because having Lindh on his knees was. He'd pulled what he said out of thin air, so as not to frighten the man away.

And a wall suddenly came down, a distinct shift in Lindh's body, protective.

Now that's interesting.

"Life before Charleston," Lindh repeated, then nodded

before pointing out the window. "There's too much to say about my life then, and we are near our destination. So let's save it for the ride."

Trillian nodded, realizing that by asking Lindh to share his life, Lindh would expect him to share a bit of his history. Maybe now was not the time to explain that he came from beneath the ocean's surface and that he was Neptune's bloodline.

They pulled onto a gravel drive and into a parking lot where a long train sat in wait. He admired the uniforms the employees wore. They reminded him of human history he'd seen in the past. His fingers itched to draw, and he automatically reached toward his bag.

Lindh laughed. "I knew you would like it. It's a step back in time, a way to view the history of the people born here in a way I'd only read about."

Odd how similar their thoughts were. Trillian glanced at Lindh and nodded. "Exactly."

He pulled his pencils out along with his notebook and quickly sketched a man from the hat he wore, wisps of red hair curling beneath its shiny embroidery, to his winsome smile. He would do his best to capture the pocket watch the man played with as he checked them in. The shiny bauble would undoubtedly have drawn the attention of Graham's youngest. He assumed Batair's young ones would also be delighted to hold it.

The man looked them both over before focusing on Lindh. "Hello, there. Nice day for a ride, yes? I've seen you before, sir."

"Yes, Michael. It's been a while." Lindh said.

"Sure has. How are your twins?" Michael looked around Lindh, no doubt searching for Lindh's children.

"Not here. I've decided to share one of my favorite things about the low country with my friend."

Michael looked Trillian over, seeing his likeness on the sketchpad. "Look at that. You know, that will cost you?"

"It will?" Trillian thought it was free to draw. He looked at Lindh and back to Michael. "How much?"

Michael laughed, and Trillian enjoyed the rich sound and deep wrinkles at the corners of the man's eyes.

"For you to have an enjoyable time. You'll have competition with him here." He nodded toward Lindh. "I think he enjoys it more than his children."

Lindh nodded shyly and looked eagerly at the train. "It was a thing of fantasies for me as a young child. Being able to enjoy the trip has always been a pleasure. Will there be hot chocolate today?"

Michael leaned close. "For you, anything."

An interesting feeling struck Trillian when the man stepped close to Lindh. All humor vanished, and a fierce need to throw the man over the vessel overwhelmed him.

Lindh smiled at Michael and pointed toward Trillian. "Just want my companion to enjoy the trip, plus the fact you have the best homemade hot chocolate I've ever tasted. Would love to serve it in my restaurant."

"That's quite the compliment coming from you, and it's definitely homemade from our chef's family recipe," Michael said, including him with a smile though it lost a little of its earlier warmth as he stared. "Seems a bit young to appreciate the finer things of yesterday."

Trillian felt his gumline itching, his fangs trying to drop in response to Michael's barely veiled challenge.

"I assure you, Michael, if I may, that I do appreciate the finer things and will continue to do so," Trillian responded, looking at Lindh and then back to his assumed competition.

Michael cleared his throat. "I see. Well, yes to the hot chocolate. Welcome to you both. Please, climb aboard and let me know if there is anything at all you might need." He nodded and clipped the tickets Lindh handed over.

"Will do. I've never been disappointed." Lindh nodded to Michael, then turned to him and said, "You'll love it."

Lindh placed his hand on Trillian's back and guided him up the stairs. When his hand fell on the curve of Trillian's ass, he gasped, the sound quite satisfying. The pants he wore were thin enough to leave little to the imagination, and the fact that he wore nothing underneath would have been easy for Lindh to detect. He smiled to himself and waited a moment for Lindh.

Lindh pressed against his back and whispered, "You are dangerous."

"You have no idea. And neither does Michael." Of course, Trillian wasn't above showing Michael how true that statement was.

CHAPTER EIGHT

Lindh found Trillian fascinating and had a hard time looking at anything but the man sitting across from him. In between conductor Michael's unusual visits, Trillian shared about his love of art, his goals for school, and his desire to take advantage of every experience while here in Charleston.

It was all new to him, all different, and it reminded Lindh of how he'd felt about the city when he first arrived, three of his Guardians traveling with him as he carried Coralia and Adamaris. They had come empty-handed, relying on past connections he'd made through the lives he'd saved years before.

It had been a fresh start with a heavy heart that had taken years to heal. The little things had stumped Lindh then. Shopping. Creating a home. Money. Finding a school for the twins when homeschooling and running the restaurant had become more than he could handle. He'd enrolled them with paperwork doctored enough to avoid questions.

His priority back then had been keeping his children safe and entertained with train rides, visits to the zoo and aquarium, gardens, and more. It had been hard for them when the holidays came around, and they didn't understand why they had no mother to celebrate. He'd told them she'd died, keeping the details vague about what took her from them. Instead, he focused on her love for them all, how they both had her smile, and while Adamaris shared her fierce temper, Coralia shared her empathy and need to help others.

He'd done his best to keep them happy. And now? Perhaps

he had someone who could do the same for him.

"Lindh?" Trillian asked as he took a sip of the homemade hot chocolate.

Trillian's lips were wet, and Lindh was hard-pressed not to lean forward and taste them.

He took a moment to glance around the car. They had great seats with a clear view as they passed by the lake and beautiful scenery. The decor was antique, and a silver tea kettle sat on the table with hot chocolate instead of tea. There was a hint of vanilla in the air, and families spread out, all enjoying the atmosphere.

Transfixed on Trillian again, Lindh responded, "Yes."

Trillian raised a brow. "Is there something wrong?" He took a crisp dinner napkin and dabbed at his lips, sitting back.

At that moment, all Lindh wanted was to play with Trillian's hair, wrap the strands around his fist, and pull the man toward him. Then dive in for a taste.

Instead, he took a deep breath. "No, nothing. Just admiring you."

Trillian blushed. Then he stood and moved to the other side of the table. "Kiss me."

Lindh looked around, but Trillian captured his chin with his fingers. His grip was tight for a smaller man, and it did something to Lindh's insides and set his heart racing.

"No, not them. Just me. I'm the only one you should care about right now." Trillian's voice resonated with need.

Lindh couldn't resist Trillian's pull and dipped his head to savor the chocolate-flavored lips before sinking his tongue within. He hummed with need, but a throat cleared, stopping him before he could take it deeper.

"Excuse me. Just checking on you two," Michael said. He refilled Lindh's glass with water. "Perhaps you need some air. The train has different levels, and each car is set in a different period. I recommend it."

Lindh took a breath to respond, quietly gasping when Trillian gripped his thigh.

"Thank you, Michael. I would like that," Trillian said.

Lindh was helpless in Trillian's wake, following him with his hand held firmly in Trillian's grasp. They walked until Trillian stopped suddenly.

Trillian looked around, pulling him into an empty berth and locking the door behind them. They were alone, and Lindh tried to step away, but his pants were opened quickly and roughly pulled down over his hips. Seconds later, his dick was down Trillian's tight throat.

His head slammed against the wall. "Shit. Oh, fuck. Trillian."

Trillian released him, the slurp almost making him come. "You looked at me like that and thought I wouldn't act on it. I had to. You wanted me to."

"I wanted to taste you, yes. Kiss you." Trillian's mouth was on him again. "Oh, fuck, Trillian."

Lindh placed his hands on the sides of Trillian's head and pushed inside. Trillian groaned, deep-throating him before shoving two fingers beside his dick, sucking them together. Then Trillian pressed sloppy spit-covered digits inside Lindh's furled hole, and he saw stars.

He tried not to scream, but it felt so good, and it had been too long since someone had taken him, given him what he needed. Trillian gripped his thigh and drank him down, finger-fucking him simultaneously. Lindh rocked back and forth, lost in sensation, completely at Trillian's mercy.

"That's it, beautiful one. My lovely Lindh. Give it to me."

Lindh moaned, trembling as he emptied, his cheeks wet with tears. He couldn't remember ever feeling so replete. So . . . *Taken.*

Lost in blissful satisfaction, his breathing ragged, he nearly fell over, but Trillian held him steady. His pants were pulled up, his dick tucked in, the zipper zipped, and the button buttoned. He opened his eyes, too overwhelmed to speak.

Trillian smiled. "There you are. Thank you, Lindh."

Lindh was taller, wider, and older, yet Trillian had mastered him in seconds.

"Thank *you*," he managed with a rough voice.

Trillian smiled and kissed him before taking them back to their table. He waved to Michael, who came over immediately. "It was a great suggestion. Thank you."

Michael looked at Lindh and then back to Trillian. "You're welcome." He sniffed, smiled, then walked away.

Lindh coughed, took a sip of water, and pointed at the landmarks of the low country as the train traveled past. Trillian listened, making notes on his sketchpad.

When Trillian took a sip of his hot chocolate, Lindh quickly looked out the window. When he turned back, Trillian gave him a knowing look.

Lindh was lost in those green depths for a moment but gathered himself. Trillian continued asking questions about the scenery they passed, and Lindh answered what he could.

When mealtime arrived, Lindh suggested items he had enjoyed. Ultimately, they decided to each order something different and share. He ordered for them and almost laughed at Trillian's expression when the meals were set on the table.

"It's what exactly?" Trillian asked.

"Shrimp and Pasta Primavera. It's sauteed shrimp with seasonal vegetables in garlic cream sauce. It's different than how I prepare it at my place, but I like their take on it."

"Hm," Trillian said. "I like my shrimp a little less done, but it smells good. And what do you have?"

"Beef pot roast."

"Cow. Like steak," Trillian asked.

"Yes, but almost a stew with vegetables, potatoes, and French bread."

Trillian nodded. "I would like that. It isn't cooked so thoroughly."

"Of course." Lindh slid his bowl over. It smelled delicious, and his mouth watered with the thought of tasting the heartiness of the dish.

Trillian smiled, wrapping his lips around the fork full. "Mm. This is very good. Would you like a taste?"

Unable to resist, Lindh opened his mouth, accepting the fork Trillian offered. "Delicious."

Trillian dug in. "Not as delicious as you, but very good."

Lindh coughed as a wave of heat crashed over him, then took a bite of the Shrimp and Pasta Primavera. It was good, but Trillian was right. It was a little more cooked than he preferred for himself. But then, he was a merman. He would have been happier pulling it from the ocean and biting the head off with his razor-sharp teeth.

Humans, though, tended to worry about food poisoning, their bodies not used to raw seafood. His restaurant served the closest to natural seafood a person could enjoy. He skirted the lines of what was allowed because, often, the ones who stopped at his place were creatures like him.

After their meals were finished, Lindh ordered his favorite dessert. He was delighted to see Trillian's delight over the banana splits. He devoured his and took care of Lindh's next.

"That was wonderful," he said after polishing off both bowls. "Thank you for the meal. I enjoyed it."

"You're welcome. I know your classes start next week, but I hope we can see each other again." Lindh spoke calmly, but he was certain Trillian could detect the yearning in his tone.

"I would like that. I'll have to focus on my classes, but I'd like to share my experiences with you. Get to know you."

There was clearly more Trillian wasn't saying, and while Lindh was curious, he was just a little afraid. Trillian was like no one he'd ever met before. Innocent one moment.

Dangerous the next.

"Good." Lindh nodded.

Lindh remained quiet when they left the train and while he drove back to Trillian's home.

As he approached their destination, he blurted, "I was married once." He hadn't meant to say it, but it just came out. "You asked about life before Charleston. I was married to my twins' mother, but one of my fellow soldiers murdered her." He had never uttered the word *murdered* to anyone, especially someone he wanted to spend time with.

"Murdered?" Trillian's voice sounded patient rather than horrified.

Lindh felt anyone else would have been appalled at the mere suggestion of murder.

"Yes." How does someone tell a lover, one who'd already sucked him dry, that the woman he loved, mother to his children, was murdered and he'd left the world he knew behind, uprooting them in favor of a fresh start?

Lindh should have stopped when Trillian remained quiet, but no. His brain refused to press pause. "She was taken from me by someone I trusted, a fellow brother. He wanted her, had fallen in love with her, and rather than let her stay with her family, he decided to take her from us."

Lindh's heart ached with the memory of loss and betrayal, and Trillian's hand on his was the only thing that kept him going. "I left everything then. Left my life there, my profession, my brotherhood, took my family, and came here."

Trillian lifted Lindh's hand and pressed it softly against his lips.

Lindh nodded, and for the rest of the ride, they were both quiet.

When they arrived at Trillian's home, Lindh waited for

Trillian to get out, but Trillian leaned over and kissed him, first on his cheeks where his tears had dried and then on his lips.

"I know you'll be busy at work, but I want to hear from you," Trillian whispered. "I have your number. I'll call. You better answer."

Lindh nodded, moaning when Trillian retook his mouth.

He waited in the car until Trillian entered his home, closing the door behind him, then drove away.

CHAPTER NINE

Lindh tidied up the condiments on the counter while Coralia sat on her favorite barstool. His nosy daughter kept her eagle eye on him as he tried desperately to ignore her.

"So, he's here again, I see. Same table, meal, and keeping an eye on you as usual. How's that going, Dad?"

She was as captivating as her mother, with honey-golden curls hanging on her shoulders and those big brown all-seeing eyes. She was hard to ignore, but he managed.

"So, when are you two going out again?" she asked.

Lindh pretended to be interested in thoroughly cleaning the oak counter, dragging the microfiber cloth back and forth. Of course, he wasn't at all focused on the gorgeous creature occupying what had become Trillian's favorite table. For weeks now, Trillian had come daily, waiting while Lindh worked, catching his attention and sharing what he was learning at school.

Lindh enjoyed Trillian's visits and looked forward to the hour when he walked through the door. He was eager to hear Trillian's stories and talk about his day.

He believed Trillian was courting him, granting him time and space, but definitely courting him. It could have been him sharing about losing Iliona, but Trillian appeared extra attentive toward him each time he visited, gifting him with a picture, a small art piece, or a story that made him smile. Flowers one time, candy another. And the sweetest smiles. Tender and delightful, sometimes cunning.

As for Lindh, he prepared special meals — squid, shrimp, oysters, all his favorites, nearly raw — enjoying the look of pleasure when Trillian ate with enjoyment. It would seem he was doing his own courting.

Lindh even gave Trillian a camera to assist him with his classes' demands and the particularities of one instructor or another. He hadn't realized how much of an investment becoming a skilled artist could be. Trillian took millions of photos and always showed them to him, pulling him close and teasing him with his scent and body's heat.

"Don't know," Lindh finally answered his daughter. "We've been talking about it."

"And?"

"You're a nosy little thing, you know that?" Lindh said.

"I am my father's daughter." Coralia picked up a carrot and drenched it in blue cheese dressing. After crunching it, she pointed the remainder at him.

"And where you're concerned, I have no choice. So give. Don't make me call Adamaris."

Adamaris. He shook his head. His son was not above pulling out all stops to get what he wanted.

Lindh threw the towel down, groaning in frustration. "We haven't mentioned any place specific. He has classes, and I have the restaurant. I'm busy, and so is he."

"There's always the weekend," Coralia sing-songed. Then, popping the rest of the carrot into her mouth, she asked, "How hard is it to go on a date with the man you can't keep your eyes off? You're over here eye-stalking him while he flips through pages of a text and munches away on whatever precious bit of food you prepared with him in mind?" She snatched up another carrot, smiling at Azizi when he replaced her snack.

Lindh thought back to his and Trillian's last date, which ended with him telling the man someone had murdered his

Iliona. Since then, though Trillian had tried, Lindh shied away. What did it say about his mental state for him to have revealed his soul to someone he barely knew the first time they went out?

That maybe I'm lonely, and Trillian is just what I need to be happy.

"Hm," Coralia dipped another carrot and then pierced him with a look.

Lindh did not like the glint in his daughter's eye.

"You want him bad, but you're scared, huh?" Once again, Coralia showed how much she was like her mother. So wise for her young age.

He was always aware. As a former Guardian, it was his skill base. He always watched, ever observant. He'd never lost that. But his lovely Iliona and his daughter seemed to have a sixth sense where he was concerned. He liked to pretend he was indestructible, but they knew . . .

As strong as he was.

As capable as he was.

He still needed someone to care for him.

And just as he'd taught his children to talk to him, to be honest, he also needed to be honest with them.

And Coralia threatening to team up with Adamaris meant the boy was on the same page. They would pull in the others, and Lindh would rather keep this away from the rest of them. He didn't want his people worried about him.

Lindh crossed his arms. "I do like him."

Fuck. Like him? I sound like a teenage girl.

Lindh more than liked Trillian. He wanted the man. He was just afraid to be with him.

"Well, alrighty then," his little dolphin said before hopping up from the bar and bouncing over to Trillian, drink in hand.

She spoke to Trillian, who looked over at him and smiled softly. Trillian nodded, and Coralia whooped loud enough for everyone to hear. His diners looked around and laughed when they saw her pointing back at him. She clapped her hands and bent to give Trillian a quick peck on the cheek.

She raced back to the bar, smiling cheekily. "Well, there you go. This evening, you're going on a date."

"I have to work tomorrow."

"Nope, I've already cleared it with your people. Haven't I?" Coralia shouted while returning to her seat.

Azizi and Edra shouted from the back, "Yes!"

"But I have nothing planned," Lindh argued.

"Well, it's a good thing you have a daughter and a son. I took care of ordering the food, and Adamaris dropped it off."

"Dropped it off? Where?"

"At your home, of course. You have a beautiful home with a lovely patio, or even your balcony where you two can sit and enjoy."

Lindh sighed, defeated. When he glanced up, he noticed someone he'd never seen before taking a seat at the back. The man was tall with long hair pulled into a thick queue. He would swear the man looked familiar but forgot about him when someone nudged him gently from behind.

"Your apron, boss?" Dorian held his hand outstretched. He raised a dark brow, his oval eyes filled with humor. "Come on. We'll take care of your baby. Take an evening off and enjoy that man waiting for you."

Lindh gazed at Trillian standing with his materials in hand. He wore a light blue flowing garment that fell to his knees and was tied with a gold belt. He looked like royalty, and Lindh wanted to be his subject. Trillian leaned his head to the side, asking without words, and the only answer Lindh had was yes.

Lindh offered to fill Trillian's glass, but the man held a slim hand up, gold bands gleaming from his fingers.

"No, thank you," Trillian said. "I enjoyed the wine, but I would rather remember the flavor of this meal and perhaps your lips. I would love a kiss."

Had he always been this shy? Not that he knew. Since he was a young merchild, he had always moved forward without hesitation. But he was in unknown territory, unsure of the next steps.

"Would you like to kiss me, Lindh?" Trillian asked.

"Yes, I would like that," Lindh said without hesitation.

"I've been hoping for another kiss for weeks now. I've enjoyed our chats, the meals with you, and sharing what I've learned. I've grown close to you in ways I haven't with members of my own family, but I've wanted — no craved — time alone with you." Trillian's gaze roamed his body before focusing on his eyes.

"I can understand that. I feel the same way, but the last time we were together . . . what I told you . . ." Lindh's words petered out, unsure of what to say.

Trillian gently grasped Lindh's hand, bringing it to his lips and kissing it softly. "Of how you lost your wife?"

Lindh couldn't look anywhere but at Trillian, offering a tenderness that he'd missed for a long time. Falling into eyes so green blades of grass would pale in comparison, Lindh nodded.

"Lindh, while I can never profess to know how deep your grief is, I can say that you should never feel you must keep it to yourself. No one should suffer alone."

Trillian's words were like a balm to his soul, giving him comfort and soothing the ache.

"It's been a long time."

"There is no expiration date on love." Trillian smiled. "I have learned my lesson on such things and am grateful to know that love is eternal."

Lindh's heart warmed with Trillian's words, and his smile

comforted him. "It doesn't hurt as much as it did. I still love her and will always love her. Yet, I feel a part of me growing closer to you. From the first moment I saw you, my spirit trembled, and my heart raced."

"And now?" Trillian asked, kissing Lindh's fingers.

"And now, the need to be inside you, or for you to be inside me, gives me life. These weeks, getting to know you, I feel closer to you. My day is empty without your visit, sorrowful without a word from you. I want to be a part of you."

"Then let me grant you your wish," Trillian said, rising and taking both Lindh's hands in his. "This meal was delicious. Now, I would like to treasure my dessert."

Chapter Ten

Trillian stared, mesmerized when Lindh's face softened, his eyes filled with so much hope and eagerness it would be hard to ignore. He wanted to do anything but ignore it. Instead, he wanted to feast on his mate.

Because that was what Lindh was . . . his mate. Lindh had no idea, but Trillian had discovered it days ago. Having reached out to Batair before his brother could call him, he'd shared how he felt.

Without giving away Lindh's name, he'd told Batair about his pangs from not seeing the man, his need to be with him every day. He shared that the mere thought of the man made his heart race and think of a future with him.

Batair had asked him when he met his mate, searching for more details, but Trillian refused to continue. Instead, he implored Batair to share about his children, asking pointed questions. It was just the lure he needed to distract his brother, who was always eager to talk about his little ones.

Now, Trillian wanted to touch, taste, and protect. He'd known Lindh was trying to keep some distance between them. Instead of pushing him, forcing him to acknowledge their bond, Trillian did his best to meet Lindh in his restaurant, where he appeared to feel safe.

Trillian bided his time, an anglerfish waiting to grasp its prey. But things had not progressed as much as he'd wanted. Yes, Lindh was more comfortable around him, sitting close to him as he showed off picture after picture, sharing his new experiences. And though Lindh smiled and fed him countless meals, another date was not forthcoming.

Until Coralia intervened.

"Where's your bedroom?" Trillian refused to release Lindh's grasp and pulled him closer instead. He would take Lindh tonight. He would bind them together forever.

"I don't know, Trillian." Lindh seemed hesitant.

"Do you want me?" Trillian asked, searching for the room himself since Lindh couldn't be counted on to help.

Lindh moaned. "More than my next breath."

Such a beautiful, strong man, wanting me desperately but so afraid to take a chance.

Well, Trillian was tired of waiting. With Coralia's encouragement, it was time for him to be an orca, not a sea anemone.

When Coralia had bent to speak with him, he'd had to laugh.

"What are you waiting on? My father wants you. Get in there and take what's on offer." Coralia had winked with a twinkle in her gorgeous eyes.

The words the lovely girl spouted had surprised but not shocked him. She appeared to be the kind of person who held nothing back.

He'd consented, and a date was planned. So no, he wasn't throwing away this opportunity. Lindh made his mouth water, and he was beyond ready to slake his thirst.

"The room to the left of the stairs. That's mine. The other two belong to the kids."

Trillian paused. "Your children still live here?" He didn't plan to be quiet or allow Lindh to be. Knowing if there would be listening ears would require him to make some adjustments.

"No, they both have their places now. However, I keep their rooms ready if they decide to stay overnight."

That solved, Trillian nodded. "Good, then. Let's go upstairs." Trillian loved Lindh's home. It felt lived in, with dark shiny wood everywhere, including the railing of the stairs. He dragged Lindh up the steps, passing photos of Coralia and Adamaris as they grew, their eyes watching him capture his prey.

Watch all you want because I will be doing very naughty things to him.

At the top of the stairs, a portrait of a happy woman with Coralia's eyes stared down at him. The oil painting seemed to glow as she sat on the beach shore, her legs covered by the ocean waves enveloping her.

She was familiar, or something about her felt like home. It nudged at him but was quickly forgotten when he felt Lindh's closeness. But he didn't let them stop there, wouldn't let Lindh second guess what they both longed for when he was this close to claiming his mate.

Merpeople were predators. They hunted. And now, Trillian felt he had been permitted to take. He not only wanted Lindh, but he needed him.

The man would be his.

CHAPTER ELEVEN

Lindh's belly fluttered with fear. He didn't want to be afraid, he had desired Trillian since they met, but they were here in his home. For him, this was more than a moment to satisfy needs. It was a turning point in his life.

The way Trillian grasped his hand tightly, pulling him into a future he hadn't expected, was beyond anything he'd dreamed of before the golden man had arrived.

Though he knew his Coralia had something to do with this, he could do nothing but thank her rather than chastise his sweet urchin.

Now, he stood naked before Trillian, his dick curved and aching, his skin hot and eager for Trillian's touch.

"You are so lovely, Lindh, do you know that? Your sweet ass, your gorgeous cock, your skin, I have no idea what I would like to touch first."

Trillian could touch him anywhere, and he'd probably go off like a ticking time bomb. He'd met Trillian's demand for him to strip as soon as they entered his bedroom without hesitation. It was as if Trillian controlled his body, and he only wished to do as the man commanded.

From the cool air hitting the tip of his cock, he knew he was dripping with precum, hungry for whatever Trillian chose to do next. "Yes."

"Yes?" Trillian asked.

"Anywhere. Touch me anywhere, Trillian. Please."

Trillian's answering smile was both sweet and wicked. He knelt at the doorway where he stood and crawled his way to

Lindh. His movements were smooth and intimidating, his gaze locked on Lindh.

Lindh was the prey, and Trillian the hunter.

When Trillian was close, he rose to his knees and licked Lindh's thigh.

Lindh hissed and rocked forward, hoping for more.

More licks came, here and there, along with nips across his sensitive skin.

"Please," Lindh begged, reaching out to tug at Trillian's hair. "Please, Trillian."

His answer was Trillian's wet mouth encircling his hard dick. The licks that had tortured him for minutes were now swiping the crown and taking him deeper. He cried out when Trillian swallowed his length, then slipped a finger in next to his cock and then plunged that sopping finger into his hole, stretching him.

The more of his cock Trillian took in, the deeper that digit went until it hit his pleasure spot, making him whimper and moan.

Trillian popped his mouth off Lindh's length and groaned. "I'm going to take you, Lindh. I have to. Do you understand this?"

"Yes, Trillian. Whatever you want. Please. Just more."

Trillian swallowed him again, throat tightening around Lindh's length, and he could have wept. Twin sharp points slid along his shaft, and he trembled, his knees nearly collapsing beneath him.

Trillian grasped Lindh's ass tightly and removed the digit that had been playing him, only to wet others as he had the first one, then spear them back into his hole. Lindh groaned with pleasure, thrusting forward. He needed this . . . craved it. Had missed being taken this way. His lovely Iliona had known of his need to be possessed, to feel her strength and know he was hers. Since then, no one had taken him as

Trillian did now.

Lindh had always been the giver, expected to dictate and dominate when his soul cried out to submit, allowed to feel and enjoy, to know he was owned. That was what he experienced with Trillian. And he'd been a fool to deny himself.

Lindh quivered in Trillian's arms, fighting the urge to come until Trillian sank his tongue into his slit and pressed a finger against that spot in his ass that made him delirious. He came with a roar, spilling down Trillian's throat and falling backward onto the bed.

He lay trembling on the bed, gasping for air, when Trillian crawled over him and kissed him deeply. He laved Trillian's mouth with his tongue, searching for bits of himself, sharing his essence with Trillian.

"So good, Lindh. Watching you lose yourself was my pleasure. Now, I wish to be inside you. Are you ready for me?"

Lindh nodded with tears in his eyes. "Yes, Trillian. Yes, anything you want from me. I would give you everything."

"Oh, you will. I'm not letting you go, Lindh. You're mine. Do you understand that? I will give you a part of myself, and you will accept it. Tell me yes."

"Yes. Yes, whatever you want to give, I will thank you for. Give me all of you." The only thing he could do was feel the searing power rushing over him from Trillian's touch.

"You're still clothed."

"Yes," Trillian said. He kissed him once more, then slowly dragged his fingers down his body, stopping at his hips. "Open your legs, Lindh."

"I want to touch you, too. Please." Lindh ached to feel the skin of the fantastic creature that made his world implode. Here he was, a merman humbled by a human, but he dared not question it because he was in a place he never dreamed he would be, the hollow emptiness he'd experienced after losing

Iliona no longer present. He still loved and missed her, but he had been given another opportunity at happiness. He would not deny himself this.

He wanted to touch, to taste. He wanted to be a part of Trillian, have Trillian be a part of him.

"You want my skin against yours?" Trillian rose to stand at the end of the king-sized bed big enough to hold them both.

Lindh licked his lips, watching Trillian as he slid his hands over his nipples and down to his renewed cock. Lindh could only nod, rising to his elbow as Trillian reached underneath his shimmery top, revealing golden skin.

Lindh squeezed himself, swiping his thumb over the tip and tasting the pre-cum he'd captured there.

Trillian grasped the edges of his shirt and pulled the fabric over his head. A groan escaped Lindh's throat when Trillian placed his fingers at his waist and dropped his wide-legged pants to the floor, revealing that he hadn't worn underwear. Instead, a band wrapped his cock against his hip, which he unhooked. Trillian's cock was gloriously long and thick, and Lindh knew it would take a bit to get him all the way in, but he was ready to try. It bounced against Trillian's abdomen as he moved back to the bed, and Lindh let his legs fall open as Trillian climbed over him.

Trillian spread Lindh's legs wider, pressing his knees against his chest. Then Trillian leaned down and slid his cool lips between Lindh's ass cheeks, licking and sucking, rimming him.

Lost in the pleasure of Trillian's mouth, Lindh wrapped his hand around his cock, rocking his ass against Trillian's face, desperate for more. He felt soaking wet from Trillian's spit, his hole stretched and ready.

"Now, Trillian. Please. I can't . . . I need . . ." Lindh begged with no thought of shame or embarrassment. Lindh needed Trillian's monster dick in his ass, desperate to be filled with

Trillian's seed dripping from him.

Trillian rose then, hooking his arms beneath Lindh's thighs, pushing him up.

"I want to see your face the first time, yes? I will have you so many times tonight, but this first time, I want to see how you change when you take me inside."

Lindh nodded and pointed toward his nightstand. "I have condoms in there."

Trillian smiled, "You told me yes, Lindh. Have you changed your mind?" He kissed Lindh's belly, licked the tip of his dick, and sucked him gently.

"Ngh. No. I'm sorry. Please. Go ahead, please!"

"I trust you, Lindh, and I promise you can trust me. This is it for both of us from now on."

Lindh's head fell back when the head of Trillian's dick nudged at his entrance. Then Trillian popped inside, Lindh's rim stretched and ready. Trillian didn't stop, didn't pause, just shoved himself all the way in, bottoming out. Lindh caught his breath before he cried out in pleasured pain.

"So good. So very tight, Lindh. My seed will travel through you, saturating you, making you mine. And one day, you will provide our gift. So many gifts. All will know you are mine." He shoved in hard, thrusting, fucking, that huge rod spearing inside Lindh, claiming him.

Lindh cried out, his ass full, his skin hot, inflamed as Trillian imprinted on his soul. "More, Trillian. More."

"Yes, Lindh. I. Will. Give. You. Everything."

Lindh's throat grew raw from screaming, his neck and shoulders covered in Trillian's bites. Tears fell on his cheeks, and his feet were in the air with Trillian's nails embedded in his skin. He rocked his head back and forth as Trillian took and took. When Trillian slid against his pearl of pleasure, he nearly blacked out. Suddenly Trillian's teeth sliced into his throat, and he opened his eyes to see Trillian staring at him, watching him while he came. He was held tight, unable to move as wave after wave of seed rushed into his body, coating his insides.

Suddenly his orgasm overwhelmed him, and he whimpered, completely at Trillian's mercy, shaking and shivering, gasping and pleading. Then he slipped into darkness.

CHAPTER TWELVE

Trillian watched his sleeping Lindh, sliding his fingers through the man's hair. His dick remained docked inside Lindh as he continued to spill his seed, feeding Lindh his essence.

He laid his hand against Lindh's belly and smiled. He would have children there soon. As his brothers had with their mates, he had planted his seed within Lindh. His mate's twins would be his, and he would love them as much as the ones he planned to give their father.

It was funny. Trillian had thought he didn't want children. Thought it wasn't in him to be a father. Then he'd found Lindh, and now he wanted to see his body swollen with his young. He would take him home to the ocean and keep him happy as they sired more together.

He ran the blood he'd taken over his tongue, savoring it. Lindh wasn't human. He didn't know what he was, but there was an otherness in his delicious taste — a flavor that called to him. He licked at the marks he'd decorated over Lindh's skin, enjoying the way Lindh moaned when he rocked forward, fucking him softly.

Lindh's purple eyes drifted open, and he smiled, looking down where their bodies joined and back to him.

"Look at you. So stunning." Trillian thrust harder, making Lindh gasp, then leaned down and kissed him.

"So good, Trillian."

"You are a gift, Lindh. Thank you for this." He fucked him harder then, wrapping himself around Lindh's body. He took

Lindh's throat into his mouth and sucked, loving the sounds Lindh made as he worked his man's body.

"Oh, Trillian."

He would never get tired of hearing his name on Lindh's lips.

Later, Trillian ran a bath for Lindh while he rested in the bed, his body good and worn just like Trillian wanted him. He would use him again several times before they parted, making sure his beautiful man wobbled a little when he walked. He wanted others to see how well Lindh was loved.

He wondered about the man as he dragged his fingers through the water.

What was he? Just looking at him had not revealed anything.

Should I ask him? What if he's trying to hide it? Would he run from me?

Whatever he was, he would be Trillian's. Aoki, Batair's mate, was a dragon. Kamau's mate Graham was human. So he would not limit himself to a genetic requirement. Lindh would be his no matter what form he took. He only needed to wait and see or convince the man he could trust him enough to share what he was.

For now, he would treasure him. Then, satisfied with the temperature of the water, he went to retrieve his mate.

After he'd finished taking care of Lindh, they slept together, wrapped in each other's arms. Throughout the night, Trillian would wake Lindh with kisses, and Lindh would take him into his mouth to show him his talented tongue.

When night turned into morning, Trillian awoke to find himself alone. Sated, he rose to relieve himself, cleaned up, and went to see his wayward lover.

He found Lindh in the kitchen, a towel wrapped around his narrow waist, humming a familiar tune while cooking at the iron stove.

Trillian watched for a moment, savoring the swiveling of Lindh's hips as he did a little dance.

"Hungry?" Lindh called back while flipping over a round disc in a flat plan.

"I am. I rather thought you would still be in bed with me. I'm not finished with you."

Lindh looked down, but Trillian saw the soft smile he tried to hide.

"I'm glad. I wanted to take care of you. One of the best ways I know is to feed you. So that's what I'm doing."

Trillian walked up behind Lindh, wrapping his arms around his muscular frame. "Thank you." He kissed Lindh's shoulder and rested his head against the curve of his back. He breathed in Lindh's scent and placed his hand over his belly.

Lindh captured his other hand and brought it to his lips, kissing it gently. "You make me happy. Last night . . . I don't have the right words. Thank you."

Trillian smiled, certain Lindh felt the smile against his skin. He was the happiest he'd ever been. Finding love wasn't even a consideration when he'd asked to come to the surface world. He'd merely wanted to learn to paint and sculpt, create worlds with his hands, but now he'd found a home for his heart.

It would take time for Lindh to accept his love and feel what he felt, but he thought they were close. There was a possibility.

"I could stay in your arms forever, Trillian, but breakfast might burn. There are plates in the cabinet over there. Get two of them. This is almost ready. What would you like to drink?" Lindh turned and planted a firm kiss on Trillian's lips, then pointed toward the sizeable industrial-sized refrigerator. "There's juice, sparkling water, lemonade, and a few other beverages. Whatever you want."

"Lemonade, of course." Trillian smiled.

Sitting and watching Lindh in his kitchen seemed surreal, domestic.

How would life be if I could always have this?

The seafood quiche Lindh had made was delicious. Trillian would probably roll wherever he went because he'd eaten two large portions — it was that good.

Lindh was wearing a satisfied smile, obviously pleased with himself. "More?"

"No, I've had enough. It was delicious, each bite more succulent than the last."

He had to smile. With Lindh showing he cared by feeding him, it was a good thing he worked out often.

"Good." Lindh looked a bit shy before asking, "Would you like to go to a movie? I haven't been in a while. I'd like to see one with you."

"Of course." Trillian would go anywhere to see anything with Lindh.

And if the endearing smile Lindh gifted him with was anything to go by, he'd given the proper response.

In the car, on the way to the theater, Trillian felt they were being watched. He couldn't pinpoint it, but there was a niggling in the back of his mind of another presence.

As they stood in line to purchase an expensive container of popcorn, he felt the strength of that awareness even greater.

"Something wrong?" Lindh asked as he handed over a card.

"No, just . . . Nothing." He couldn't shake the feeling and knew better than not to trust his instincts. As a creature of the ocean, self-awareness was the difference between life and death. But he refused to lose the progress they'd made so far. It was their night, and whatever or whoever was out there didn't matter.

CHAPTER THIRTEEN

The movie was great. Lindh loved movies with unbelievable human characters performing superhuman feats. Costumes, superpowers, and humor were the clinchers for a great evening for him. Spending his evening watching the movie with Trillian was beyond his dreams.

They shared the massive container of popcorn, feeding pieces to each other while holding hands. Lindh felt like a younger, happier, freer version of himself. It had been years since he'd enjoyed time with someone who made him smile as much as Trillian, who listened to him go on about his restaurant and trying new recipes. Trillian didn't just pretend to be interested in what he had to say, hoping he would bed him. Instead, his green eyes watched him intently, focused on every word. It was a heady feeling to be someone's single focus.

He loved the feeling. And he loved Trillian. He had no idea when it had happened. Perhaps it had always been there, but he recognized the feeling. He was both happy and afraid. He didn't know how to tell Trillian.

Did Trillian feel the same?

Did Trillian need him the way he needed Trillian?

When they left the theater, he spotted the same person he'd noticed in his restaurant, someone both familiar and not. His Spidey-senses activated, or more aptly, his Guardian skills. He looked around to see if there were any others and saw another man off to the left, leaning against a car.

It could be nothing, but he was having doubts. Trillian

stiffened beside him, which only confirmed that he should be concerned. He wrapped his arm around Trillian's waist, drew him to his car, opened the door, and placed him inside gently.

When he looked up again, searching for the two he'd noticed earlier, neither was there. Pulling his phone out, he called his men.

Dorian answered on the first ring. "Lindh?"

"I think I'm being followed. I spotted two."

"Where are you? Do you need us there?" Dorian's voice filled with concern, letting him know he would be ready at a moment's notice if needed.

"I don't think so, but I feel they are brothers."

"What makes you think so?"

"They were familiar. One was at the restaurant the other night and here at the movies tonight. And Dorian. I think Trillian noticed it, too."

"Think he knows something?"

"Not sure, but I need to get him home. I won't chance his safety."

"Understood. Check-in later."

He clicked off and got into the car.

Lindh and his Guardians had been through too much together for him to try something like this alone. They shared all, and no matter what, they stood as one. When he got home, he would immediately send a message letting his team know he'd made it in safely.

"Lindh," Trillian said with some reluctance.

"Who are you, Trillian?"

"What do you mean?"

Lindh faced Trillian, reaching out and pulling him close. "I mean, that those were Guardians out there . . . Shadows. And I haven't seen them in over fifteen years. Not until you came into my life. So, who are you?"

"Can we go to your home?"

A pleading filled Trillian's eyes, a look of worry and apprehension Lindh had not seen on the man's face before.

"We can, and when we get there, we're going to talk."

"Yes, Lindh."

As he approached his home, he glanced around, checking the surroundings. The Shadows had apparently not found him here. He would have noticed them, felt their presence. He tried to think of how many signs he'd missed that Trillian wasn't human but a merman like him. And not just any mere merman. Someone up the line, someone with a personal entourage of Guardians.

He pulled into his driveway, turned off the car, and exited. He fired off a message to Dorian before he strode around to the other side, opening Trillian's door. Reaching in, he tugged Trillian out of the vehicle and against him. Then he kissed him hard, wanting him to feel his fear, his frustration, and the hunger he couldn't deny. He slammed the car door and dragged Trillian with him, climbing the stairs quickly and striding into his home, ensuring the door was shut and secure behind him.

Taking Trillian into his arms, he kissed him again, sliding his hand along his sides and cupping his ass. "Talk."

"I can't think when you're touching me like this. Kissing me. I can't tell if you're angry with me or if you want to fuck me."

"Both, except I want you to fuck me." Lindh kissed Trillian again before taking him to his den, where they could sit. He needed to keep his hands off Trillian, but the more he was with him, the more he couldn't resist him. There was a fire burning inside him that was only growing stronger.

Mating.

"Do you feel it, Trillian?" Lindh almost whispered.

"Yes, I do." Trillian reached out, placing his hand over Lindh's belly. "Within you is a part of me."

Lindh's eyes widened as he absorbed Trillian's words. "You gave me your young?"

"Ours. You carry my line, Neptune's line."

Lindh groaned, and his blood ran cold, "Trillian."

"Lindh, I couldn't help myself. It was too strong, and I shared my seed with you knowingly. I had no idea you were a merman and that your body would accept so easily. But I won't lie. I hoped. When we return to our world, we can have our family there. This will only be the first of many."

Lindh sat on his plush couch, his head falling against the back. "I can't believe this. You're one of Neptune's grandsons — part of the royal line. I'm a guardian carrying Neptune's line, with Shadows stalking us. Do you have any idea who killed my wife, Trillian? Why I live here and have for more than twenty years away from the ocean that gave me life?"

Trillian eased to his knees in front of him. "No. I remember you mentioned she died, but not what killed her."

"Who. It was a who. Years ago, I was a Guardian with two beautiful children and a loving mate. But a fellow Guardian wanted my Iliona for himself, coveting her kindness and dedication to her family. He wanted the love she showed me, someone he deemed unworthy of her, for himself. And when he couldn't turn her eye, he killed her. And do you know what happened? I was told to remember that the brotherhood of Guardians was stronger than the bond between a merman and his mate, that while it had been a horrible accident, the brotherhood was worth more. An accident? Like him using his trident to rip my beautiful Iliona apart could have been forgiven. So I killed him. And then, I left them all behind."

Trillian was quiet, his tearful eyes watching him closely as he lost it. It all happened years ago, but right then felt as if it was yesterday. Seeing the Shadows, knowing they were here for him, somehow broke him. He would not relive that nightmare. He could not.

"And here you are, someone really fucking important, so

vital that I'm afraid to know your identity. Did you know who I was? Was this some type of plan to make me love you, want to have this happiness with you only so you could help them drag me back to the sea?" Lindh's throat hurt from the volume of his cries, tears streaming from the corners of his eyes.

"No, Lindh. No. I promise you I had no idea. I thought you were human. My brother is a Guardian, and I didn't recognize any of that in you. Batair always taught me to be observant."

Lindh sucked in a breath. "Batair? Batair is your brother?"

"Yes. You sound like you know him."

"Know him? The man is my best friend. How did your name never come up? How did I miss this?" He stood, grasping at the strands of his hair as he paced. "My best friend is a Guardian and the brother of my lover. And wait . . ." Lindh spun around, facing Trillian and touching his belly carefully. "I feel it." He glared at Trillian. "You claimed and mated me. I wasn't listening. The life within is already flourishing." He flopped onto the couch.

"Yes. And now you will be mine forever and carry my young. We will add more. I want a big family, a dwelling filled with our children. You will bring Coralia and Adamaris, too."

Trillian knelt before him, his forehead against Lindh's knee. "You are the mate I never knew I wanted, Lindh. My heart races when you are near. Waiting for you to want me as much as I want you has been torture. Forgive me for doing whatever I could to have you in my life forever."

Lindh shook his head slowly, too overwhelmed by this man and what their futures could hold. "I never wanted to go back, Trillian."

Trillian looked up, gazing long and hard into Lindh's eyes. "I understand, but I must. I promised to return. I gave my word to my grandfather and my family. I came here to learn to become an artist and what it was to create. And while I have what I've always wanted, what I've always needed is right here in front of me. Please don't try and ask me to leave that behind, to leave you behind. I can't do that."

Trillian was the grandson of Neptune, a member of a family he'd sworn years ago to protect. He was Batair's younger brother. And here he was, kneeling between Lindh's legs, asking for a chance at a future in a place Lindh never wanted to see again.

CHAPTER FOURTEEN

Trillian blamed his family for this. Batair had promised to leave him alone, let him experience the surface world without interference. They'd shared a message or two, but his brother stayed mostly silent. While Batair had kept his word, the rest of his family had apparently had enough of wondering where he was and sent Shadows, the elite guardians of their world, to investigate.

And very nearly cost him the love of his life.

He looked up, Lindh's head back, his neck the only skin he could see. But Lindh touched him, combed his fingers through his hair, and breathed deeply in and out.

"I'm sorry about your fears, which is probably a nightmare for you, but I'm not sorry about finding you or having you in my life."

Lindh sighed. "I don't know what to say, Trillian. My heart beats for you. It has from the moment I met you. You made me breathe again. But this? I don't know if I can go back."

"Please, Lindh," Trillian begged.

There was a knock at the door.

Lindh stiffened. "I feel them out there. They know who I am, what I am. I draw them like a beacon. Brothers."

But Trillian heard a voice call out, recognizing it as one of Lindh's people. He got up and went to the door.

They were armed, all three, tridents in hand. The Guardians were a people of their own. Strong and magnificent. Trillian stepped back and allowed Lindh's soldiers entry.

Fists to their hearts, each bowed their heads, not to Trillian as was customary but to Lindh, who stood to receive them.

"Thank you, but I don't think it will come to this, or at least I hope it won't." Lindh looked at him, moving into his outstretched arms.

"It won't. I can promise you this, Lindh," Trillian murmured.

"Whatever you need, Tetra, we are here," Dorian said.

"No longer Tetra to you, Dorian. We are family. The title of lead Guardian no longer divides us."

"We are honored to be your family, Lindh, but you have always been Tetra to us and will forever be. We serve at your word," Azizi said.

"I'd rather you be at my side," Lindh smirked.

Dorian smiled, then nodded. "We can do that."

"Yes," the others agreed.

"But, again, it will not come to that." Trillian wrapped his arms around Lindh, rubbing his flat belly that would eventually distend with their child. "It mustn't. Lindh carries my young. He and I will soon have a family of our own."

Three pairs of eyes looked from him to Lindh and down to where his hand rested possessively.

"Tetra?" Dorian questioned.

There was no mistaking the happiness in Lindh's voice as he answered. "Yes, I have been claimed and mated."

Trillian smiled at his words, ready to take his mate again, his dick already hard.

But it would have to wait. Lindh's front door flinging open, revealing a phalanx of Shadows who would have to be dealt with first.

"Our great Neptune has commissioned us to return you to your home, grandson of Neptune," the Tetra announced.

Trillian didn't recognize the man standing before him in full armor, helmet, enchanted gloves, and trident. Still, he knew the attire of those responsible for his family's safety.

Had it been a year? He was promised a year. Thinking back, he'd been here less than nine months. Surely his grandfather wasn't going back on his word.

"I was promised a year," Trillian said confidently.

"Yes, sir, but our Lord Neptune grew worried that you have forgotten your purpose and requested you return home."

"Forgotten my purpose?"

The Tetra of the Shadows dipped his head and then looked meaningfully at Lindh.

"Ah. He knows then," Trillian said.

"He does," the Tetra nodded.

"How long have you been following me, sending tabs back to my patriarch?"

"Neptune has eyes everywhere. He knows all and has watched from afar, but with your conquest, he has determined that a year is no longer required."

"No." Trillian would not be pushed or forced. He refused.

The shock on the Shadow's face would have made Trillian laugh if he weren't so angry. Unfortunately, he needed more time to convince Lindh to come home with him. True, Lindh carried his young, but as their gestation period was shorter than humans, they might need time to figure out how to hide the treasure Trillian had planted there.

"No?" The Tetra frowned.

"Exactly. I was promised a year, given his word. Therefore, I will stay here for the year and return as agreed. Hopefully, I will not arrive alone."

Trillian turned to Lindh, drawing him close. Lindh's eyes fluttered shut before Trillian kissed both lids tenderly.

"We have been sent to return you, willing or not." The Tetra took a step, then stopped.

Lindh raised his head, his grin ice cold, the man he had once been coming to the surface as he took his stance, lifting his hand. His armor flew to him, trident in hand he pushed Trillian behind him. "You may try, but you won't live to share the story. I have been in this situation before. I lost my love once. I promise you it won't happen again."

Love? Lindh loves me.

The Shadows spread out quickly, tridents ready, but Lindh's soldiers were faster, easily unarming each of the Shadows and taking them down with a speed that surprised Trillian.

Lindh pointed his trident at the head of the Tetra. "My mate has given his answer to your king. He will stay with me until the year he was given is finished. Only then will he return."

"Though you left your calling, Tetra Lindh, I am proud to see it is still in your blood. You will always be a Guardian," said the Tetra of the Shadows.

"Yes, but I won't be yours or even Neptune's. The only one of your royal line whose call I will answer is the one who stands beside me. I will never be at the beck and call of those who failed me."

"We didn't fail you. It was so many years ago, and the entire truth was hidden from those then."

Lindh shook his head, and Trillian reached for him wrapping his arms around him.

"Leave. I am not going with you. I know my purpose, and he lives and breathes beside me. Rise and go." Trillian's tone was resolute.

The head of the Shadows stood, signaling to his men to rise with him. "You caught us unawares," he rumbled to Lindh.

"That is your failing. Not mine," Lindh growled in return. "You heard him. I suggest you heed his words."

When Lindh's men moved aside to let them pass, they walked out the door, but not before casting one more glance in Trillian's direction.

"I understand you are doing the job you were sent to do.

This is not your fault, " Trillian said, his words both kind and powerful. "But I was given a promise. I also made one, which I intend to keep. I am only insisting that my grandfather keep his." He refused to argue with the men chosen to heed Neptune's command. "You won't be blamed for this. On the contrary, I will ensure no blame falls upon you."

The leader nodded, but then he paused. "We knew of you, of your loss, Tetra Lindh. We felt your pain then."

CHAPTER FIFTEEN

The entire moment was surreal. Lindh's men stood before him, facing the Shadows and armed to the hilt, ready to intercede again if necessary.

How had they even made it to my home dressed in their guardian gear?

Surely someone would have noticed two tall men and a woman carrying tridents and dressed in shimmering armor, helmets scored with the symbols of their people, and strips of clothing adorning their hips and waist.

Naked, other than their chest plates and sporadically placed slivers of cloth, each was a magnificent specimen of merkind, and they belonged to him. He was no longer the Tetra he'd been, no longer the soldier of so many years ago, but they had chosen to stand by him rather than surrender him and his mate to the Shadows.

He could barely breathe as the Shadow Tetra stared him down with an intensity that touched his core, speaking words that chilled him to the bone.

"We never wanted you to leave, but we were ordered to give you the time you needed to heal. It is not only the princes of Neptune that we were trusted to guard."

Lindh waited for the rage to come, anger at the injustice of his loss, the words of apology that never came, the pain from being forgotten.

He felt nothing but regret.

"You could have done something then," he said, an ache in his chest.

"Our arms were tied, but we understood your need for retribution. We allowed you to take Falon's life in payment for what he did to your Iliona. He was not allowed an honored burial. Instead, the Shadows fed his torn body to the sharks."

"A brother?"

"Any guardian that would do such a thing to the heart of another was not worthy of being a brother. He was churl to us."

"Churl?"

"Yes, a defilement to our people, as you know. He and his line were erased. Those who chose to cover his crimes suffered his fate as well."

Lindh felt the wetness on his cheeks and leaned into Trillian's hold. "All this time? You let me think that I was alone."

"We let you heal. You needed to leave, to strike out on your own. You couldn't serve. You needed exactly what you have done. With us, you would only have second-guessed our motives for years. And while you didn't trust us and cast us into your past, you still cared for others and your soldiers. And we watched from a distance."

Lindh took a cleansing breath. "And now?"

"Now, our prince has chosen you as his own. But he still has a promise to keep. What will you do when he must honor his word?"

"We will make that decision, not you, Shadow." Trillian practically spat the words. "You've said enough. It's time for you to go."

The Tetra's icy blue eyes scrutinized him, taking his measure. "We will go for now, my prince." He bowed respectfully to Trillian and turned back to him. "Tetra Lindh." He placed his fist over his heart and nodded before turning to go, his fellow Shadows in his wake.

"Well, fuck," Edra said once the Shadows had disappeared into the night.

"Yes. That exactly." Lindh's voice sounded rough to his own ears. The evening had been filled with surprises for everyone involved, especially him.

He shook his head. The Shadows had supported him all this time. He had never been alone but just hadn't known it. And they'd only revealed themselves now because of what?

Had they wanted him to know they were there? That it was time to move on and leave his fears from the past behind? To live again?

Was he ready for that? Yes, he was more than ready. Inside him was a new life. He placed his hand over the warmth he already felt blooming there and smiled.

"Tetra Lindh." Edra caught his attention. "I believe it is safe for us all to go and give you and your mate time alone."

Lindh nodded. "Thank you, Edra. I am grateful to all of you. You're my family."

"And you are ours, and we are happy for you. Whatever your decision, we will always follow you." Edra nodded and led Dorian and Azizi out the door, each bowing as they passed him.

Did Lindh feel so near tears because of the hormones of carrying this young one? Trillian wrapped his arms around him, and though his mate was smaller and appeared more delicate, he had an iron strength that couldn't be ignored.

He turned to face Trillian and leaned into Trillian's welcoming strength, the safe shelter of his embrace.

"You are mine, Lindh. Now and forever. You are my place of sanctuary. I know you didn't expect this, had no idea what would happen the day you met me, but every second with you has been a gift to me."

Lindh breathed deeply, savoring Trillian's scent, his warmth.

Trillian kissed him, lips soft on his skin, hands resting over his belly protectively. "You carry a part of my very soul. I want to be wherever you are."

"At the cost of your promise? Your word?" Lindh knew Trillian couldn't just renege on what had been asked of him. But was he ready to return to the ocean? To see his home? To introduce his Coralia and Adamaris to the life he'd known before, one they knew nothing of? He'd kept their origin a secret for years, never believing he would have to face his past. He'd remade himself — left that world behind.

Or had he been lying to himself all along? Someday they would find a mate of their own. Then what? He'd taught them nothing about what to expect, how to live beneath the surface. As far as they knew, they were both allergic to the ocean, the water dangerous for their skin.

Lindh had lied to his children, telling himself he'd done it to protect them. In reality, he had been defending himself, living in a world of his making. He'd kept the two people he loved more than life itself in the dark while living in the past.

"Lindh?" Trillian sounded worried.

He focused on Trillian, wondering how long he'd been lost in thought. "I need to tell Coralia and Adamaris the truth."

"Yes, but it doesn't have to be tonight. Let me hold you, make love to you. Then we can both fill them in together tomorrow."

Trillian's hands were already roaming Lindh's body, gently teasing him here and there. Lindh's cock filled, and he trembled with need.

"There you are, my love." Trillian slipped his hand into Lindh's pants, fisting his member.

Lindh moaned. "Trillian." He would have been embarrassed by the needy whine in his voice if he wasn't rocking desperately into Trillian's grip. Before he realized what was happening, his balls roiled and tingled, signaling he was about to come.

Trillian worked fast to open Lindh's pants, then dropped

to his knees and wrapped his lips around the head of Lindh's dick, his hands grasping the shaft and balls. When Trillian swallowed him to the base, applying exquisite pressure, Lindh roared, mouth open, head back, eyes closed as he shivered his release. Finally, when his legs couldn't hold him anymore, he fell into Trillian's waiting arms.

"I have you, Lindh. Let's clean you up so I can show you how happy I am to be your mate."

CHAPTER SIXTEEN

Trillian rubbed Lindh's leg soothingly, noticing the tremble in his mate's thigh.

"So, wait a minute." Coralia calmly raised her hand as if sitting in a class review for a final exam. "We're what now?"

"Merpeople," Adamaris answered, slowly tilting his head.

Coralia nodded, her expression thoughtful as she processed what had to be the craziest news of her twenty-four years. "Nope. Not getting it. Like, in the ocean?"

Trillian and Lindh sat with the twins at the family table in the restaurant's kitchen, their private family spot. It said a lot that the four were meeting in what was like a second home to Lindh. While Trillian was honored to be there, his insides quivered with worry.

What if the two people Lindh valued most in the world wouldn't accept him? What if they blamed the truth on Trillian as if he'd somehow bewitched their father?

But when Lindh's hand slid into Trillian's, he held on tight, ridding himself of the constant worry gnawing at his mind. They were here together. He would be here for his mate, faithful that they would overcome the omission of truth Lindh had committed because of fear. He would stand by his mate to help explain if necessary.

Adamaris cleared his throat. "So, is that why we don't swim in the ocean? We're not allergic to ocean water. We belong in the ocean." He leaned back. "How long would you have kept this from us, Dad? If Trillian hadn't come along, would you have told us the truth?"

"Yes. One day."

Coralia shook her head. "No, Father. You should have told us before. Part of me might think I'm losing my mind or that this is some over-the-top prank you're trying to play. But I've always thought—Adamaris has, too—that we were different from our friends. More instinctive. And it is odd how the ocean seems to call to us."

Lindh dropped his head and sighed. "I failed you."

"No, you don't get to say that. You lied to us but did it to protect yourself and us. I can't believe I'm talking about this like this is normal, as if I've already accepted it as fact. But haven't we always suspected, Adamaris?" Coralia looked at her brother.

Adamaris nodded. "Yes. And when we thought to ask you, we somehow worried if this connected to our mother. And rather than see you heartbroken, we said nothing. But we have many questions, and now that the subject is open, we want answers."

The twins were taking this better than Trillian expected. He slid his thumb over Lindh's knuckles, offering him support. It wasn't his place to speak. This was between his mate and his children.

Lindh squeezed back, then began telling them of their mother. The one who lived beneath the ocean surface with him who hadn't always walked on two legs as the portrait in Lindh's home might have suggested. She was a mercreature just like him. He told them of being a Guardian and a Tetra, calling his soldiers into the kitchen and reintroducing the men and woman who would give their lives for him and the family they had protected for years.

Coralia's eyes teared up and she gripped Adamaris's shaking hand when Lindh spoke of the day he'd lost their mother and of his pain. He told them of killing the man who should have been a brother, who'd chosen to lust after another's mate. How she had refused him but then was murdered for her refusal. He described how he'd killed the man, and when it seemed no one would be there for him and his family, he'd taken his babies and gone to the surface world. But he hadn't arrived alone. His soldiers had traveled with him, choosing loyalty and friendship over the comfort of home.

Coralia sniffed. "So much time." She looked at Trillian, and while her smile was watery, it was also welcoming. "Thank you."

"Yes, thank you," Adamaris added. "Because of you, we will have a chance to know another part of ourselves. Who we truly are."

"Yes, about that. There's something you should know about me." Trillian took his turn, telling his story and sharing his secrets.

"Wait. Neptune is your grandfather." Coralia stared with wide eyes.

"Yes," Trillian answered.

"And he allowed you to come here and live for a year?" It was Adamaris's turn to gape.

"Yes."

"But you're not going back?" Coralia questioned.

"No. I am, and I hope I can take your father with me. He carries my young."

Coralia shook her head. "I need a drink. I don't usually because I only get a quick buzz, but I'm willing to drink the whole bottle if it helps right the fuck now."

Adamaris leaned forward, peering at Lindh's belly as if he could see a sign of life there for himself. "You're pregnant?"

Lindh nodded.

"Merpeople, both men and women, can carry young. I must be honest with you. I knowingly impregnated your father."

"You fucked my father and got him pregnant on purpose?"

Adamaris growled, glaring at him.

Trillian could see the flame of his people within Adamaris's eyes. How they'd hidden it from themselves, he had no idea.

"Yes. I wanted your father to have my child, to be locked to me forever. So I opened myself and fed him my essence. His body accepted me, and he is mine.

"It is the way of our people. We operate more on instinct. I waited but took him when I finally had my chance."

"Fuck, you're pregnant, Dad? There's a baby inside you," Coralia whispered. "Trillian's baby, my brother or sister."

Lindh sighed, "Yes, and I am happy. I can feel my connection growing with our child."

"How long."

"Days."

"In days, you can feel something?"

"Yes, without a doubt. It's very much like Batair has described to me."

"Uncle Batair."

"Has given birth to each of his and Aoki's six children. And knowing Aoki, he'll more than likely try for another after the seventh is born. Batair is happy and glows with it. I want that. I want this baby. I want Trillian."

"Oh, wow. I just . . . I thought they had surrogates, ones they visited, spent time with, and then returned. Oh, I'm an idiot," Coralia seemed confused, but she was trying.

It was all they could ask of her.

"What now," Adamaris asked.

"Well, Neptune is petitioning for my return, but I will remain here as promised and cultivate my relationship with my mate and, hopefully, his children. Perhaps help teach you two to love the creature within that has been calling to you, no doubt. As your father carries my young, he cannot take a different form, but I can. I can also teach you how."

Both children shared a look of longing and then beamed their hopeful gazes at their father.

Coralia nodded. "We would never want to do anything to hurt you, Father, but we have both felt like a part of us was missing. To learn about that would be an answered prayer."

Trillian looked up at Lindh and squeezed his hand. "Let's help them with that, my love."

Lindh nodded to his children. "I owe you this."

"Yes, Dad, you kinda do, and we love you, so we forgive you. I know that's probably why we can accept the craziness you just dropped on us," Adamaris said before downing the glass of wine in front of him.

"Well, how about today, then?" Trillian asked.

That night, Trillian welcomed Lindh into his arms. The joy of having his mate next to him unfurled within him, and he felt whole.

When he'd decided to visit the surface world to study the human artistic skills he'd admired so greatly, the idea of finding his mate here had not crossed his mind. And now? Now, as he caressed his mate's belly, drawing his fingers over the roundness there, he was happier than he'd ever been. Had he wanted to be a father? No. Yet here he was, looking forward to tiny fingers and iridescent scales. Would their first child have Lindh's gorgeous eyes and Trillian's waist-length hair? Would it be a girl, fierce and powerful like Coralia, or a boy who enjoyed painting like Trillian?

"What are you thinking about?" Lindh whispered.

"So many things. Chief among them, our young. Your son and daughter, soon to be mine, are amazing. I didn't know your Iliona, but I can see her in those two, how loyal they are to you. The light they both have in their eyes even though Adamaris is quieter and more watchful than his father. Given time and training, you know he could have been a Guardian."

"Yes, that's true, but I would rather see what he chooses to become. Our destinies have been so entwined with what others have chosen for us. My son and daughter can determine their future for themselves. It's what has made my efforts worthwhile for me. "

"I understand. My life is at the behest of Neptune. With my brothers having made choices no one expected, there was more focus on my return. But to be honest, I want to. I want to share what I've learned with our people at home. I want to bring back the light I've found here so others may see its glow."

And he wanted to show off his beautiful mate. Some people back home would be shocked by Trillian claiming a mate for himself, especially one as strong and powerful as Lindh. And then to have that Guardian gift him with their child? It was a dream he had never fathomed.

He smiled as he thought about his adventures with Adamaris and Coralia earlier that evening.

They walked the shore with Adamaris and Coralia, who faced the ocean for the first time without fear of the water. Instead, they both stood there, holding hands, breathing in the ocean air. After a shared look, they stepped out into the water.

The two stood knee-deep in the water, naked and comfortable in their skin, neither shy about their bodies. It took very little encouragement for them to accept the changes that slowly manifested. The surprise on their faces and the glow that emanated from them both made Trillian's fingers itch to capture the image on canvas to last a lifetime. The moonlight that danced over the water, the gentle cresting of the ocean waves, and the sound of a guitar in the distance made for a perfect moment.

Every merperson had different colored scales, from vivid hues to dark and rich ones, from jeweled tones to ones that resembled the rocks on a shore.

Trillian figured Coralia and Adamaris shared the coloring of their mother. She must have been extraordinary, because looking at the two of them took his breath away. Their scales were variants of gold, green, blue, and red, coasting down their arms, over their chests and breasts, cascading across their shoulders, and rippling down their spines until they rounded their hips and legs. Legs that quickly morphed into tails before both he and Lindh pushed them further out into the water.

They laughed and played, diving in and around, swirling beneath the water and spraying out with a flip in the air, only to repeat it several more times.

Lindh watched his children with a soft smile on his face and hands resting against his waist.

When Trillian realized it would be a while before getting the twins back, he settled Lindh on the shoreline and joined them. It was equal parts amazing and terrifying. Here was the family he never knew he wanted, and his fear that he wouldn't measure up to the person they needed was crushing. But he let all of that go and enjoyed playing with his new son and daughter.

When they finished late into the evening, they returned home. Coralia and Adamaris retired to their childhood rooms, still excited but tired from accepting their merforms. Trillian led Lindh to his bedroom, helping him get undressed and into bed, then climbing in beside him.

Trillian hugged Lindh closer. "They are stunning, your children. Thank you for this evening."

Lindh turned to him, eyes wet with tears. "Thank you, Trillian. I had no idea I could be this happy when I met you. I think I'd given up on the possibility, content with ensuring that Coralia and Adamaris were taken care of, wanting for nothing. So I opened the restaurant and made it a safe haven. And then, you walked in. And my whole world changed."

"For the better?"

"Gods, yes. Now, I look forward to each day I spend with you. Especially now. You've given me hope, Trillian. Joy. And now? Life. Thank you."

Trillian sank into Lindh with his hand covering his mate's belly protectively as he slowly loved him with deep kisses and tender touches. However, their orgasms were upon them quickly, and rather than rise to clean his mate, he lay twined with his love. Sticky and wet, they were coated in each other's juices.

Sated.

Together.

Whole.

Epilogue

"Are you ready, Lindh?" Trillian's voice shook with his nerves as they approached the beach. Months had passed, and it was time to take his mate home.

Lindh was round and beautiful, and Trillian couldn't wait to get him home where he would give birth to their future. Lindh's happiness with the pregnancy helped calm his anxiety over parting with his restaurant. The manager-chef he had hired for his place was efficient and welcoming and would have Batair there to guide him. Batair was happy to help, too excited for Lindh to have the happiness he deserved if not biased since Lindh's mate was Trillian.

Trillian had met with Batair to share his new status, surprised to be warned by his brother to care for his mate or else. Lindh's heart was priceless to Batair, and the two of them had become brothers. It was not lost on Trillian that their relationship, based on their shared callings, had progressed to an unbreakable bond, one that Trillian would do everything to support.

Trillian knew Lindh would want to return to the surface to visit Batair and check in with Coralia and Adamaris. And his heart was in the restaurant, which many had come to know as a safe haven, a home. Trillian knew it would be difficult for Lindh to leave the place behind, so he made sure the person they hired could love Iliona's namesake almost as much as Lindh did.

The man's name was Tony. He had four children who would help him. They varied in age but were all a joy to meet, each topped with the bright orange color of their father. Trillian and Lindh had enjoyed a meal prepared by Tony with love and comfort, which included the types of food Lindh usually served and plentiful seafood. Tony's little ones were disorganized until Adamaris popped by and moved to help with eyes bright and welcoming.

Tony fit, and Trillian wasn't sure, but he thought he noticed a tad of interest from Tony as he glanced at Adamaris.

Was Lindh completely ready to leave the home he'd claimed for many years? Not entirely, but Trillian understood Lindh's wariness. His fears. And he would be there for him.

"Yes, I'm ready. There may still be days when I remember losing my Iliona and vowing I would never return home. But now? I don't know what to feel, but I'm thankful to be at your side even if your Guardians surround us."

Apparently, Neptune wasn't taking any chances. They stood surrounded by guardians and the Shadows who had stormed Lindh's home. Yet Trillian didn't feel any hostility. No aggression. Instead, he sensed warmth and respect.

A voice called out from the sea, and immediately the Shadows and Guardians divided until there was a path to the ocean for Trillian and Lindh to take.

"Step forward, Tetra Lindh, Guardian of Neptune and sire to my line. Present your mate, grandson of Neptune." Neptune's voice echoed across the water.

"How does he know," Lindh whispered to Trillian.

"How he knows everything. He is a god. He is always listening and has more eyes than we will ever know," Mazu said as she stood waiting, smiling gently at Lindh.

Lindh took a deep breath, his chest rising and falling. If Trillian listened closely, he could almost hear Lindh's heart race. He took Lindh's trembling hand and brought it to his lips, kissing his knuckles gently.

"Hello, Grandfather. Mother. I bring to you Tetra Lindh,

retired Guardian of Neptune and sire to the first of my future children."

"I am pleased to welcome home one of mine. Thank you for returning to us, Trillian, and bringing us such a treasure. Know, Tetra Lindh, that you were never lost to us. You were given time to heal. Come to us and live among your people." The ocean waves crashed in response to Neptune's words.

They had both said their goodbyes to their family. Batair had chosen not to come at Aoki's request, staying behind to keep his family safe and away from Neptune. Trillian understood. Neptune could be demanding and was not above capturing his family by any means, dragging them down to him.

Coralia and Adamaris would visit one day. But for now, they would remain and earn their degrees. The restaurant would go on in the care of Tony, who smiled when he cooked, whistled when he cleaned, and watched over the restaurant's diners as if they were family. He'd brought in cooks, ones he trusted. Iliona's Sea Haven was in good hands. Just as Lindh would be in Trillian's.

"We will go first, Tetra Lindh," Dorian said.

Lindh's soldiers had chosen to return with him. They'd all sat together two evenings ago in Lindh's home, the table covered with plentiful platters of raw fish, lobster, seaweed, and pasta. It was a celebration for all of Lindh's family — *their family*, for that night.

Edra stood, placing her fist over her left breast, pledging herself to Trillian. Dorian and Azizi were quick to follow her. His eyes teared up when all three knelt, bowing their heads toward him. They didn't have to. They were Lindh's, but they apparently trusted him, and he refused to fail them. He would make them all proud, especially Lindh.

He stood, going to each one and hugging them tightly before helping them to stand.

"You are my family. As you have been Tetra Lindh's, you are now mine, and I will always honor this, your gift to me."

Now, Dorian, Azizi, and Edra flanked him and his mate, armed and ready as they entered the sea. His mother embraced first him and then Lindh, bending to kiss Lindh's belly. He could feel Mazu's happiness, and he was eager to show everyone the prize he'd captured for himself.

Because Lindh was indeed his prize, his treasure. He'd come to the surface world for his dreams to be fulfilled. And now? Now, he had a mate, a child, and a family to care for below.

Months later, Lindh rested in bed, his baby against his chest, holding her tightly. Little Iliona had come into the world, kicking and screaming, and he had immediately held her to him, feeding her, sheltering her, his heart beating hard as tears fell from his eyes.

His little Iliona was a gorgeous creature, covered in shimmering scales with tiny pink lips. Her eyes were purple like his, but he could already see that her hair would be white blonde like Trillian's.

He listened to the chants of their people as they celebrated the new life . . . his little Iliona. Since her arrival, gifts had been left for the youngest of Neptune's line, and mothers and sires stopping by to whisper blessings and offer aid.

The people's joy at his and Trillian's happiness, the genuine welcome they gave as Trillian presented his family with his head held high, had gone a long way to calm his fear of returning.

And now, with Trillian holding him tightly as he held their Iliona, he could wish for nothing more.

His heart was full of love.

105

Life's greatest masterpiece.

OTHER BOOKS BY DEJA BLACK:

A Place For Dreams
Getting There
Stumbling in the Dark
They Called Him Nightmare

Broken
    Broken Bones
    Broken Pieces
    Broken Promises
    Broken Dreams

Children of the Sun
    Flirty and Red

Men of Neptune
    Song of the Siren
    Guardian's Prize

Tengu Goblins
    Challenge the Sun (Part of the Winter Magic Anthology)
    Say Yes (Part of Autumn Feast Anthology)
    Wink (Part of Spring Fever Anthology)
    Beyond the Veil (Part of Summer Heat Anthology)

About the Author

Deja Black had fantasies of men loving men, men who felt strongly, loved hard and needed a hero. Then one great day, she came across a book and discovered the world of m/m writing, encountered others who shared her obsession as much as she did, and found a world where she could not only be accepted for the lives and loves she envisioned, but she could create them too. So why not? Why not take the stories she would write and throw away as a teenager, grow them, dream them, and make them a reality where she could know her characters, let them live their story, and make them real for someone else? And she did. Now, with the support of her hubby and some intense time management, she is learning to balance her family of two energetic children and a White's Tree Frog at home, along with the many students she counsels each day with her passion for writing what she loves to read.

Deja is always interested in connecting with new people who also share her love, so please feel free to contact her at:

Facebook: www.facebook.com/deja.black.69

Website: dejablack.net

Twitter: @DejaBlack69